Human behavior was certainly a mystery...

"Do you want me to tuck you in?" asked Jay.

"No, I'm fine. You've been so kind." Shanna lifted her chin bravely. Her temporary blindness kept her from seeing the man who had saved her life. What color were his eyes? Was his expression as firm, as gentle, as caring as his voice? When he was around she felt loved, protected...but was her judgment as cloudy as her eyesight?

"You sound as though you're expecting me to bill you for services rendered," Jay said huskily, touching her cheek. "I'm someone who cares for you, Shanna, and if you think I'm going to waltz out of your life, you're way off base."

Dear Reader,

The word *angel* conjures up chubby cherubs or wizened old specters, not men who are virile and muscular and sinfully sexy. But you're about to enter the Denver Branch of Avenging Angels and meet some of the sexiest angels this side of heaven!

Whenever there's injustice, the Avenging Angels are on the case.

Leona Karr brings you the third irresistible angel in *The Charmer*. This time, the angel really *is* a cherub! Little Ariel is determined to both play matchmaker and help solve a murder!

I know you'll love Ariel—and all the Avenging Angels coming your way through May. Don't miss any of this superspecial quartet!

Regards,

Debra Matteucci
Senior Editor & Editorial Coordinator
Harlequin Books
300 East 42nd Street
New York, New York 10017

The Charmer
Leona Karr

Harlequin Books

**TORONTO • NEW YORK • LONDON
AMSTERDAM • PARIS • SYDNEY • HAMBURG
STOCKHOLM • ATHENS • TOKYO • MILAN
MADRID • WARSAW • BUDAPEST • AUCKLAND**

To Susan W. Ray
Our special friendship was meant to be.

ISBN 0-373-22366-8

THE CHARMER

Copyright © Leona Karr

This edition published by arrangement with Harlequin Books S.A.

® and TM are trademarks of the publisher. Trademarks indicated with ® are registered in the United States Patent and Trademark Office, the Canadian Trade Marks Office and in other countries.

Printed in U.S.A.

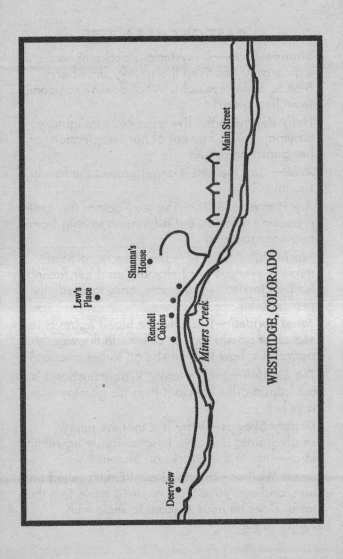

Main Street

Shanna's House

Lew's Place

Rendell Cabins

Miners Creek

Deerview

WESTRIDGE, COLORADO

CAST OF CHARACTERS

Shanna Ryan—A mysterious accident had temporarily deprived the spunky strawberry blonde of her eyesight. What doesn't someone want her to see?

Holly Ryan—Is the five-year-old's imaginary playmate just a figment of her imagination, or her guardian angel?

Ariel—Can the littlest angel protect the family she loves?

Jay Harrison, M.D.—The sexy doctor has quite a bedside manner. But is he open to help from heavenly sources?

Marla Dillard, nurse—The cheerful, efficient nurse is everybody's helpmate, and her feelings for Dr. Harrison's father are more than strictly professional.

Janet Rendell—The talkative blond Texan is in search of gossip for her column in the weekly paper. Just how far will she go to get a scoop?

Ted Rendell—Janet's lanky, likable husband is cut from a different cloth than his gossipy wife. Isn't he?

Deputy Skaggs—Why is it that the pudgy, sandy-haired detective is so curiously unwilling to investigate the attacks on Shanna?

Lewis Walker—Shanna's aunt Emma relied on him, and everyone thought she'd leave him the farm. Does he have a score to settle with Emma's real heir?

Chapter One

Midnight darkness seeped into the mountain valley, and the furtive figure skirting the old Victorian house was scarcely more than a flickering shadow in the moonless night. Tall lodgepole pines stood like giant sentinels on the rocky hillside, their thick-needled branches moving slightly in a hushed stillness.

A small porch lamp sent a radius of light down the front steps of the house, vaguely illuminating the far corners of the front porch but too feeble to reach the side of the house, where a late-model Ford was parked.

A crunch of hurried footsteps on the gravel broke the night's stillness. A pair of gloved hands reached out and slowly and silently lifted the hood of the car. Muffled sounds of labored breathing and scraping metal were carried away on the soft night breeze. A moment later, retreating footsteps and a satisfied sigh left a hushed silence on the hillside.

There, it was done. And no one the wiser.

SHANNA LOOKED OUT the kitchen window and smiled as she watched her five-year-old daughter roll pebbles down the sloping hillside behind the house. A bright morning sun washed ponderosa pines and quivering aspen leaves with green-gold tints, and a cloudless April sky spread above distant peaks like a baby-blue blanket. A quiver of relief went through her. It was going to be all right. Holly had been jerked around from army base to army base all of her short life. It was time her child had a permanent home. Shanna lifted her chin even as an inner voice nagged, *Are you sure you want to live in an isolated mountain community like this?*

No, I'm not sure at all, she admitted to herself. A hundred times, she'd gone over the options facing her as an army widow since her husband's accidental death. She'd married Allen before she even finished college, and her experience in the work field was zip. She had only two options: get a menial job and make her widow allotment stretch as far as possible, or try to do something with the property that she had unexpectedly inherited from her elderly Aunt Emma.

She had to admit that her first view of the two-storied house set against the rugged mountainside had been less than reassuring. To a woman used to compact army housing, the Victorian-style mansion looked quite formidable. She had despaired of it ever seeming like home, but after only a week in the house, she'd fallen in love with the high ceilings, ornate woodwork and wide halls that echoed as she walked across wide-planked oak floors. The idea of turning the place into a mountain bed-and-breakfast seemed a natural. She could hardly wait to begin picking out paint colors and wallpaper patterns.

Even though her Aunt Emma had kept up the property, Shanna saw a dozen improvements she needed to make before the first guest arrived. Her mind raced ahead with all the things that needed to be done. Then she caught herself. One thing at a time.

She swept a strand of reddish blond hair back from her forehead. Today they'd make the eighty-mile trip into Denver and stay overnight with one of Aunt Emma's old friends, who had made them welcome when they arrived in Colorado. The shopping list she'd made would take a whole afternoon, and she had promised to take Holly to see a Disney movie.

As she watched her curly-headed daughter bobbing happily around on the hillside, her eyes grew misty. Holly was a pretty child, with warm brown hair, alert blue eyes and a cute nose that wrinkled when she laughed. She was laughing now as if someone were playing a game with her. Ariel, thought Shanna. Her daughter's imaginary little friend. Holly had developed her pretend playmate when she was about three. As far as Shanna could tell from Holly's chatter, Ariel was a kind of older sister, about ten years old, with blond hair.

Shanna was well aware that some parents tried to discourage this kind of fantasy, but she'd decided to play along with the idea. What harm could there be in Holly pretending that she had someone to play with? She'd outgrow the need soon enough as she got older. Shanna turned away from the window, deciding to let Holly stay outside a few more minutes before calling her in to clean up.

"Mine's faster than yours," squealed the little girl as she watched a round rock about the size of a baseball roll down the hill.

Ariel laughed, resisting the temptation to send a ripple of air behind her stone to hurry it along. She'd created the game to keep Holly entertained in the strange new mountain setting. A five-year-old could be trying at times, especially when her life had been turned upside down. Being a Guardian Angel was a challenge sometimes, particularly when Holly was scared or lonely and even a best friend couldn't make it better.

"You win," Ariel agreed, and was rewarded with a broad smile from Holly. Ariel's heavenly existence had not included the responsibilities of Guardian Angel—until Holly. Although delighted with the special charge, she was still a novice in carrying out the earthly assignment. Ariel was content to materialize for Holly's eyes only. Like best friends, they played together, talked together, and, when Holly woke up in the night, frightened or lonely, Ariel was like an older sister always there to comfort her. Everyone tried to convince Holly that her playmate was just pretend and when she told them exactly what Ariel looked like, they just sighed and patted her head. Sometimes Holly's mother teased her about talking to herself but the two girls just smiled at each other. Adults didn't know everything.

A few minutes later, the back door of the house opened and Shanna called, "Holly. Time to come in."

Holly scrambled to her feet. "Come on, Ariel. Race you to the house."

"You're on!" Ariel laughed and let the little girl get a head start. Holly's brown curls danced around her face as her little legs covered the ground in a rollicking gait. Ariel skimmed lightly over the ground behind her, her silken blond hair fanning out in the air.

"I beat Ariel," Holly gasped as she bounded into the house.

"Whoa!" laughed Shanna as she steadied her. "You're lucky you didn't fall on your face running down the hill like that."

"Ariel wouldn't let me," Holly said smugly.

The vote of confidence worried Ariel. In all honesty, she hadn't quite mastered split-second interference tactics. She sometimes practiced on Jiggs, Holly's little brown dog, by giving him a shove off the chair and then trying to catch him before he hit the floor. Most of the time she was quick enough. Most of the time.

"You can come to Denver with us," Holly told Ariel. "Mama's going to take us to a movie, but you'll have to pay your own way."

Shanna overheard the remark and laughed to herself. Nothing like making imaginary friends go dutch. She gave her daughter an affectionate pat on the behind. "Go wash up, Holly, and put on the yellow pinafore dress I laid on your bed."

Her daughter scampered up the stairs. Shanna lingered a moment in the kitchen and gave it a cursory look. An old coal range stood against one wall like a monster ready to belch black smoke, but Aunt Emma had installed a modern four-burner electric stove beside the range. Thanks heavens! Used to the compact kitchens of base housing, Shanna was still dismayed by the size of the room. Unhandy, old-fashioned working counters seemed a long way from the refrigerator and stove. She'd be walking miles back and forth between appliances and cupboards unless she installed an island worktable in the middle of the floor. Shanna frowned. All the changes couldn't be made at once. Maybe the kitchen would have to wait until—

The ring of the front doorbell broke into her mental prioritizing of improvements.

Who could that be? She hadn't had any visitors the few days they'd been in the house. Jiggs beat her to the front door, woofing furiously. He was a small dog of undetermined parentage with caramel-colored fur and floppy ears.

Shanna peeked through a small beveled-glass window set in the front door and saw a rather blowsy-looking woman with frizzed short hair bleached an uncertain blond color. Shanna scooted Jiggs out of the way with one foot and opened the door.

"Hi. I'm Jan... Janet Rendell. My husband, Ted, and I own the fishing cabins along Clear Creek just below your property," the woman said in a marked Texas drawl. "Makes us neighbors, you know. Thought I'd best drop by and say howdy." She wore tight jeans that molded her full hips, a fringed shirt that strained at the front buttons, and tasseled cowboy boots. Shanna decided the woman looked as if she might have a horse tethered nearby. "Hope I didn't catch y'all at a bad time."

"No, not at all. Come in." Shanna stepped back, wishing she looked a little more presentable. In another few minutes she would have been cleaned up and dressed for town. That morning, she'd thrown on a pair of old sweatpants and a long-sleeved shirt because the night chill lingered in the house. She'd already discovered that temperatures fell drastically after the sun went down in the high mountain valley.

"Things are still a mess," Shanna apologized. "I'm not very far along in unpacking."

Janet's round eyes were openly curious as they registered Shanna's reddish blond hair and traveled over her nicely endowed bustline, slim waist and slender legs. "Maybe I can give you a hand."

Shanna didn't respond to the offer as she led the way down the hall to a small sitting room adjoining the downstairs bedroom that her aunt had used in her later years. She was uncomfortably aware of the littered appearance of the room. She hadn't had time to clear away her aunt's knickknacks and dust the rosewood furniture, which included some lovely antique pieces.

The way her visitor was gawking around the room made Shanna think that she hadn't been in the house before. "Did you know my Aunt Emma?"

Jan shifted the tooled leather bag she had hanging from one shoulder. "Everybody kinda knows everybody in this small town, but your aunt kept to herself. I reckon I should confess right up front that I write pieces for the weekly *Westridge Courier*." She gave a hearty laugh. "People say I'm nosier than a badger poking his nose in a rabbit hole."

"You're a reporter?"

Jan settled her buttocks in a Victorian wing chair. "Well, now, I'd say more of a columnist." She laughed again. "Folks have a natural curiosity about things and people. And I figure it's my job to give 'em something interesting to read about. Right now, you're the one who interests me."

"I can't imagine why," Shanna said, suddenly feeling slightly off-balance, the way she did when she unwittingly let a salesman or religious fanatic into the house. "I assure you there's nothing about me that would make good copy."

"You're a newcomer to Westridge," said Jan, as if that explained everything. She reached into the leather bag and pulled out a small spiral notebook and a pen. "How do you think you'll like living in an isolated mountain community like this?"

Shanna hesitated and then said firmly, "I don't think the isolation will bother me. I've spent most of my married life being pretty much confined to an army base."

"Where are you from originally?"

"Hartford, Kansas. I met my husband when he was stationed at Fort Riley and I was a sophomore at Kansas State. I'd never been out of the state until I married Allen."

"And you think you'll like living alone in an old rambling house like this. Pretty lonely, I'd say."

I'm used to living alone, Shanna thought silently. Allen had been gone months at a time, and even when he was assigned to a home base, he'd spent his free time at the club or playing with his army buddies. It seemed to her that she'd never really shared her thoughts, her dreams or her inner self with him. But that part of her life was over, and she certainly wasn't going to share it with this avaricious small-town gossip columnist.

"How long have you been divorced?" Janet asked.

Shanna blinked. "Divorced?" she echoed. "I'm a widow. My husband, Major Allen Ryan, was killed in a helicopter crash several months ago."

Jan's pen flew. "Oh, I didn't know. So you were an army wife. Traveled all over the world, I bet."

"Not really." Shanna sighed. Propaganda made living on various bases sound romantic, when most of the tours were a painful adjustment for every member of the family. "We spent two years on Okinawa. The rest of the time we were stateside. Holly was born in Fort Benning, Georgia, and my husband was reassigned every year since her birth.'' Shanna moistened her lips. "When my aunt left me this property, I decided to settle down here with my daughter.''

"A widow." She eyed Shanna. "A classy-looking gal like yourself living alone in a place like Westridge will cause a few tongues to wag.''

Shanna hesitated. She wanted to put an end to this so-called interview, but she had the feeling that the woman would make up any facts she didn't have, and if so, there was no telling what she would put in her column. Shanna worried about false rumors getting into print. Sooner or later everyone would know her plans for the house, and once the workmen arrived, she'd undoubtedly be a topic of conversation whether she wanted to be or not.

She was a little wary about the twist Janet might put on everything she said. There was something about the woman that reminded Shanna of a crocodile with its jaws open. Common sense told her not to get too close or cozy with Janet. They might be neighbors, but never friends.

"I've decided to turn the house into a bed-and-breakfast,'' explained Shanna in a businesslike tone. "I've been told that Westridge is about the right distance from Denver for a weekend stay.''

Janet frowned and pursed her red lips. "Don't know who told you that. Westridge isn't on the tourist track. Never has been. You'd do better to sell the property and put your money into something else.''

"But I don't want to sell the property.''

"Then you must have plenty of money to sink into the place. Did your aunt leave you some assets besides the house? Rumors were that the old lady had a lot of money hidden under her mattress.''

Shanna wasn't going to grace such rumors with a reply. It wasn't anybody's business how she was going to pay for the renovations.

At that moment Holly yelled down from upstairs. ''Mommy! I can't find my shoe.''

Thankful for the interruption, Shanna stood up. ''I'm sorry you're going to have to excuse me. I'm getting ready to make a trip to Denver.''

''Another time, then,'' Jan said with a practiced smile that didn't quite reach her eyes.

Not if I can help it, Shanna thought as she bid her neighbor goodbye. She closed the front door with a little more firmness than was necessary. She certainly hoped Jan Rendell wasn't representative of Westridge's welcome committee.

Shanna hurried upstairs to get herself ready for the trip into Denver, and had just changed into a pale cream summer skirt, paisley blouse and sandals when the doorbell rang again. She groaned. Had that woman come back to ask even more questions?

Shanna peered out the door glass and saw a young girl in her teens standing there in fringed shorts and a halter top. Long strands of blond hair fell limply around her scowling face as she jabbed the doorbell impatiently. A black-haired boy about a head taller shuffled nervously behind her. He wore overalls with one suspender hanging loose and a shirt that had grease stains all over it. His hair was as long as the girl's but not as clean. Both of them stiffened and glared at Shanna as she opened the door.

''Is my mother here?'' demanded the girl, her scowl deepening.

"Your mother?"

"Janet Rendell. She said she was coming to see you."

"Oh, she left a few a minutes ago."

"What did she tell you?"

"About what?" Shanna asked, puzzled.

The two teenagers exchanged quick glances.

"Drop it, Billie Jo," the boy growled. "I told you it was a stupid idea."

The girl gave a toss of her lank hair. "Never mind," she said abruptly. Before Shanna could ask any questions, they turned, bounded down the front steps and climbed into an old model car of an uncertain blue color. Neither of them looked back at the house as the boy gunned the backfiring car down the narrow dirt road in a swirl of dust.

What was that all about, Shanna wondered as she closed the door. Weird, that's what. She certainly hoped the rest of her neighbors weren't as peculiar as the Rendells. The way the young people had glared at her had brought a prickling up her spine. The newspapers were full of scary stories about wild and hostile teenagers. She was left with an uneasy feeling and wished that she'd been more settled before meeting her neighbors.

Shanna settled Jiggs on the back porch with food and water. Then she yelled up the stairs, "Come on, Holly. Let's go."

Holly bounded down the steps at a wobbly speed that threatened to plunge her headfirst if she tripped on the worn carpet runner. *Careful, Holly,* Ariel admonished, floating along beside her, but, as usual, when the little girl didn't want to do as Ariel said, she just pretended she wasn't there. And that was that.

Being a Guardian Angel certainly had its challenges, Ariel had decided more than once.

Shanna locked the front door and took Holly's hand as they went down the flight of wooden stairs. Ariel swept out of the house beside them, but instead of floating into the back seat as she usually did, Ariel stopped in midair before she reached the car.

Something was wrong.

There was a dark energy around the car.

Evil.

All of Ariel's angelic telepathic perceptions fired with a warning blast. Her powers as a Guardian Angel were not all-knowing, but she recognized a dark force surrounding the car.

What did it mean? What should she do?

Ariel had no vision of the future, because the capricious free will of mortals made human life impossible to predict. She had to deal with human activities as they occurred. If the situation warranted, she could materialize, either as herself or in another living form, and become visible to everyone or only one person. But what good would any of those options do in this situation when she couldn't identify the threatening danger?

As Shanna started to drive away, Ariel swooped into the back seat. She was an unseen presence except to Holly, who turned around and giggled at her. Ariel's primary charge as a Guardian Angel was staying close to the little girl. The drive to Denver involved a mountainous road hugging craggy cliffs, with sharp curves that twisted along a precipice that dropped off into chasms hundreds of feet below.

Shanna had only driven a few hundred yards away from the house when Holly squealed, "Look, Mommy, a horse."

Shanna slowed down, half expecting to see Janet, but the rider was a man whose tall, lanky frame sat the horse well. He disappeared through the trees toward the fishing cabins set along the creek. "Ted Rendell?" wondered Shanna. She hoped he wasn't as abrasive as his wife—or as hostile as his daughter and her boyfriend.

DR. JAY HARRISON GLANCED out a window of the tiny Westridge Clinic and saw Shanna's car as it slowed down for a couple of jaywalkers and a stray dog strolling across Main Street.

Who's that? His quick glance registered a pretty light-haired woman behind the wheel. She laughed as she waved the ambling pedestrians on, and then said something to the bobbing head of a child sitting beside her. He'd never seen her before. In the two months he'd been relieving his father as an itinerant doctor in the Colorado mountain community, she hadn't shown up at the clinic or crossed his path the two days a week he spent in Westridge. She must be a tourist just passing through. She certainly wasn't the kind of woman anyone would overlook.

"That's it for today, Doctor," said his nurse as she came back into the examination room. Marla Dillard was a plump, attractive woman in her mid-thirties, spry and efficient. Her round face easily creased into a smile. Jay's father thought she was about the best nurse around, and Jay suspected she spoiled his dad shamefully. Marla eyed him frankly as she quickly put the examination room back in order. "Not much to keep a city doctor like yourself busy."

So far today they'd had a few people with colds, a baby with colic, and one broken arm. Nothing serious enough to keep anyone overnight in the clinic or to send to Denver by ambulance. Jay took off his white coat, hung it on a coatrack in the corner and slipped into a tailored brown jacket, a shade lighter than his thick dark hair and tailored to accent his broad shoulders.

I bet you're anxious to get back to your New York hospital."

"I don't know if *anxious* is the right word, but I'll admit I'm ready to plunge back into the fray."

"How is your father? Will Dr. Harrison be able to take over for us again when you leave?"

"He made it through his bypass surgery nicely. Chances are good that he'll be able to resume his practice...and his commitment to this clinic. He really enjoys spending time in Westridge. Frankly, I think he'd rather live in this small mountain community than in Denver. I've been talking to him about retiring, but he's stubborn and thinks fifty-eight is too young."

"He's a fine specimen of a man," Marla declared, and then colored slightly.

Jay hid a smile. So that's the way the land lay. He'd suspected as much from some of the things both Marla and his dad had said. Apparently the two of them had spent a great deal of time together outside clinic hours.

"Are you enjoying his mountain cabin? Your father always spent as much time at Deerview as he could."

"Well, one night a week is enough for me. Too damn quiet." Jay laughed, and the dimpled cleft in one cheek deepened. "I need some police sirens and honking taxis to put me to sleep. I get mighty restless with nothing happening."

Marla cocked her head and fixed her clear hazel eyes on him. "I think Dr. Harrison was hoping you'd like Colorado enough to stick around permanently."

Jay shook his head. "I'm a city boy. I'm only taking a short leave of absence from Manhattan General because of my father's health, but when he improves, I'll be on the first plane back to New York." He picked up his medical bag. "Well, I guess I'll be on my way. See you next week."

"Give your father my best," Marla said as she walked to the door with him. "Tell him fishing is good in the creek. Better hurry and get his line in the water before I catch all the big ones."

Jay laughed. "I'll tell him."

Westridge had started out as a silver mining camp, and as Jay drove west on a narrow two-lane highway, he wondered how wagons had ever made it over the craggy ridges that lay between Denver and the small mountain town. Twisting mountain curves kept his shoulders tense, and he would have preferred the strident horns of a dozen taxis to the wailing banks of wind sweeping down from high, jagged peaks.

As he drew in several deep breaths and tried to relax, he wondered how many more times he would have to make the weekly trek from Denver. His father's general Denver practice had been put in the hands of a colleague, but Pop had persuaded Jay to fill in for him in the Westridge clinic until he could resume the two-day mountain practice. Jay could understand why his father enjoyed the slow-paced, low-key clinic. Most of the practice catered to good ole boys who liked to shoot the breeze while the Doc stitched them up or patients who needed medication for common aches and pains. His father had always preferred a small-town practice and couldn't understand why his son had chosen to be on the staff of a New York hospital.

When Jay put his life on hold in order to help out his father, he'd hadn't planned on staying more than a month. Even though he could extend his leave from Manhattan General, he was filled with a restlessness to get back to the exhausting grind that kept his personal life on hold. Since he'd been in Colorado he'd had too much time to think. Too much time to be bitter. He'd needed work to drown out the memory of a dead-end marriage and the betrayal of someone he had trusted. Even now, he couldn't believe what had happened.

The ugliness of his divorce was at the front of his mind when he saw someone ahead, waving from the side of the road. He slowed down and saw that it was a blond-haired girl about ten years old.

He slowed to a stop. She jerked open the door. "There's been an accident. A car went off the road. I'll show you where . . . hurry."

"How far?"

"Only a couple of miles." She eyed the medical bag in the seat between them as she climbed into the passenger seat. "Good, you're a doctor."

Jay nodded as he gunned the car forward. His hunched shoulders and the white-knuckled grip he had on the steering wheel told Ariel he wasn't used to mountain driving. He kept his eyes fixed on the twisting road, and several times he came dangerously close to the edge as the car skidded around a curve.

"There!" She pointed ahead.

Jay couldn't see any evidence of an accident and knew he would have driven right by the spot without knowing a car had plunged off the cliff at that point. He braked to a stop on a narrow shoulder of the road. About two hundred feet down the rugged slope, a blue Ford Taurus perched precariously on an outcropping of rocks.

"A mother and her little girl are trapped inside."

His breath caught in a quick intake. Carefully walking to the edge of the drop-off, he could see that the ledge holding the car could give way from its weight at any moment. Jay ran back to the car. Thank heavens his father had installed a cellular phone in his car, thought Jay as he called 911 and reported the accident. "Get a tow truck and ambulance up here fast."

He hung up, grabbed his doctor's bag and turned to the little girl as she stood beside the car. "You stay here."

Ariel nodded, but as soon as his back was turned her human form disappeared in a burst of light. Jay paused at the edge of the drop-off and searched for the quickest way down to the car.

He discarded the idea of going straight down. A zigzag descent came to him as the only safe way to navigate shelves of rock and rough, sloping ground. Filled with a sense of rising urgency, he lowered himself over the edge.

Loose rocks slipped away from under his feet, and he caught himself by grabbing a scrawny scrub oak bush that was growing up between cracks in the shelves of rocks.

Ariel hovered unseen in the air beside him, bombarding him with telepathic warnings.

Not that ledge.

Jay pulled his foot back from stepping on a piece of sandstone, suddenly realizing that somehow it wouldn't hold him.

Turn back the other way.

Cautiously, he turned in a different direction, descending downward, creeping over boulders sticking out of the cliff's face and obeying orders in his head.

Watch that rock.

Sweat beaded on his forehead as he made his way down the sloping mountainside, foot by foot, rock to rock, and step by step.

Like a flicker of light, Ariel whipped back and forth, knowing that even her best efforts might fail if he ignored her warnings. Humans could be downright stubborn at times. In spite of all kinds of intuitive warnings, they set their jaws and did exactly what they knew they shouldn't.

A rising sense of urgency sent Jay scrambling down a rocky crevice made by snow runoff, and in his haste, his doctor's bag slipped out of his hands. In a split second, Ariel swooped downward and threw up a force field just as the medical kit was about to sail out into midair. It slid a few feet below Jay and stopped. He breathed a prayer of thankfulness as he retrieved the bag.

After what seemed like an excruciating eternity, his feet finally touched the rocky outcrop holding the car above the chasm below. The way the car hung on the edge, Jay feared that the earth could drop out from under it at any moment.

He gingerly approached the car. He couldn't see any movement through the spiderlike web of the cracked windshield, but he heard muffled sobs.

Someone was still alive.

"I'm coming," he called.

The car had landed so that one of its front wheels dangled in midair, and Jay feared that just opening one of the doors might dislodge it from its precarious perch. His fear was confirmed when he reached the car and a heard a sharp crack of rock under his feet as if the whole ledge was threatening to give way.

Hurry, hurry, lashed the same inner voice that had brought him safely down the mountainside.

He gingerly opened the door and saw a woman slumped over the steering wheel. A little girl huddled in the front seat beside her, and when she saw Jay, she sat up and reached out her arms with a whimpering cry.

"It's all right," he soothed as he took her in his arms. As quickly as he could, he carried her a safe distance away from the rocky ledge and set her down on a small mound of hard dirt and stones.

Even though the child's body shook with sobs of fright, she seemed to be perfectly all right physically. No blood, no broken bones, no bruises. A miracle, he thought. "Stay here like a good girl while I get your mother."

With a whisper of wings, Ariel surrounded Holly with protective warmth and touched a kiss to her forehead with the softness of a summer breeze.

A mounting urgency engulfed Jay once again as he returned to the car. He recognized the young woman as the pretty strawberry blonde who had caught his attention when she drove by the clinic. Her head rested against the steering wheel, and her slender form was limp and still. He reached for her hand and felt for a pulse. Thank heavens, she was still alive.

He unfastened her seat belt, and as he began to gently draw her out of the car, he prayed that he wasn't causing more injuries by moving her. Another crack of crumbling sandstone told him that he had no choice. He couldn't chance leaving her where she was and having the car plunge the rest of the way down into the deep canyon.

She was light in his arms, and as he cradled her against his chest, a faint scent of perfume lingered in her hair. Even with blood covering one side of her face, he could tell that she had delicate, well-balanced features. Long lashes fringed her pale cheeks, and lustrous honey-red hair framed her oval-shaped face.

When he laid her down on the ground near Holly, she groaned.

"Mommy," sobbed Holly. "Mommy?"

At the sound of her daughter's voice, Shanna's eyelids fluttered. Fringed by golden lashes, her clear blue eyes were so lovely that Jay was startled by the impact her gaze had upon him.

"Holly, where are you?"

The little girl scooted closer.

Shanna turned her head and winced. "I can't see you. My eyes!" she cried in terror. Everything was indistinct and cloudy, as if she were at the bottom of the ocean. A swath of gray lay like a curtain across her eyes.

Jay put his hands on both sides of her head like a vise. "Don't move." He took out his stethoscope, listened to her quickened heartbeat. He gently lifted her eyelids and flashed the small pen flashlight into her eyes.

She could barely make out a human form as he bent over her. "What is it? Where am I?" Panic rushed through her with the force of a torrent.

"There's been an accident. Try to relax. I'm a doctor and an ambulance is coming." His deep masculine voice flowed over her. "Tell me where it hurts."

She raised her hand. "My head."

"Easy." He pulled her hand back down.

Her voice rose in panic. "Why can't I see?"

"Sometimes a blow to the head affects vision." He didn't think she'd suffered a skull fracture, but he had no way of knowing how bad her concussion might be. And without an ophthalmoscope, he couldn't tell what lay behind the cornea of her eyes. He speculated that there had been a vascular breakdown, causing excess fluid to the eyes. "We'll know more when we get you to a hospital."

"Holly?" The pain in Shanna's head was growing and exploding behind her eyes. "Honey, are you all right?"

The little girl only gulped back tears and whimpered.

"She's fine. Hardly a scratch," Jay assured Shanna. Holly whimpered again, and he added, "She's just frightened."

Shanna didn't know who he was or how he had come to be at their side. His hands were sure and gentle as he staunched the bleeding wound above her right temple. He cautiously checked her arms and legs, and she heard him let out a relieved breath. "Good. No broken bones."

She shivered, and he quickly took off his coat and laid it over her. Even though the April sun was shining brightly, the crisp mountain air had a chill in it.

"Thank you," she murmured.

He worried about the faded color in her lips. Damn, he wished he had some blankets. He didn't want her to lose consciousness and go into shock. Where in the hell was the ambulance? His 911 call should have brought help by now. In the city—but this wasn't the city, he reminded himself. He hoped to God they didn't have to wait for help to come all the way from Denver.

"It's going to be all right," he said as much to himself as to her.

Shanna was grateful for the warmth of his coat. She could vaguely see a shadowy outline and nothing more as he bent over her. A faint masculine scent matched the texture of the cloth, and she felt the warmth of his breath as he leaned over her. His voice was a lifeline, and she grasped at the assurance of his commanding tone. She reached out and caught his arm. "Don't leave."

"I won't." He slipped his hand into hers, and she tightened her fingers around it like a child afraid of the dark. "It's going to be all right," he told her. Even in this dire situation, she was unbelievably attractive. Her lovely, natural strawberry blond hair was a shade he'd never seen before, and her complexion was flawless. "Help's coming," he promised. "I—"

He broke off as a deafening rumble and sharp crack of breaking stone filled the air. He jerked his head toward the car and stared in disbelief as the shelf holding the car dropped away. Clouds of dust rose in the air as it plunged downward amid a cacophony of shattering glass and screeching metal. An avalanche of rocks carried it to the bottom of the ravine, and an instant later the car burst into flames.

Jay's mouth's was dry as he looked below. Even though he had been expecting something like that to happen, the shock of knowing how precarious every moment had been brought beads of sweat on his brow. Thank God he'd gotten them both out of the car in time.

"What is it?" cried Shanna. She had felt the earth vibrate, and her nostrils filled with dust as she gasped for breath. Her unfocused eyes jerked around. "What was that noise?" Her nails bit into his hand. "What's happening?" Her voice rose. "Tell me . . . !"

"Your car just plunged the rest of the way down the mountainside. When you went off the road, by some miracle the car got hung up on a rocky ledge. I was able to climb down to the car and get you and your little girl out of it before . . . before it went over."

"Oh, my God," she breathed. Horror brought a trembling that nearly made her teeth chatter.

"You're safe enough now. We'll just wait until help arrives. Then we'll get you to a Denver hospital." He decided to try to keep her talking. Somehow fears lost some of their power when they were verbalized. "Do you remember going off the road?"

Her lips trembled. "Yes."

Probably driving too fast for the conditions, he thought. Hell, that road was a disaster waiting to happen. There were a dozen hairpin curves that could send a car spinning over the edge in the blink of an eye.

"The car . . . something went wrong with the car."

"What?"

"Something went wrong with the car," she repeated, frowning as if trying to draw something out of her memory.

"Brakes?"

"No, not the brakes. The accelerator...it...it stuck."

"The accelerator stuck," he repeated, trying not to sound skeptical. Was she lying? Did she feel guilty? Guilty enough to try to pretend that it wasn't her driving that had caused the accident? "Are you sure that's what happened?"

Her voice rose hysterically. "The foot pedal was jammed down to the floorboard. There wasn't anything I could do."

"Easy, easy," he soothed. He didn't want a hysterical woman on his hands.

Ariel knew that Shanna spoke the truth. Now she knew what the dark aura around the car had meant. Someone had deliberately tampered with the car. She'd been aware of an evil presence and lingering menacing vibrations but had realized too late what the dark aura had meant. Someone had meant for the car to go off the road with Holly and her mother in it.

"You must have seen what happened," Shanna insisted in a voice trembling from pain and fear.

"No, I wasn't close to you when it happened. A young girl stopped my car on the highway a few miles from here and showed me where you'd gone off the road."

"Ariel told me she was going to get help," Holly said solemnly.

"But honey...but she...she couldn't," her mother stammered. "Ariel is Holly's little imaginary friend."

"Imaginary? She's waiting in my car right now," Jay insisted.

Holly looked at Ariel, who was visibly perched on a nearby rock. "But—"

Ariel winked at Holly. It didn't do any good to argue with adults. They never understood.

Ariel knew that her duties as a Guardian Angel were limited. Her assignment was to remain close to Holly and protect the child as best she could, nothing more. A separate echelon of Avenging Angels handled assignments that exposed evil and brought wrongdoers to justice. If she wanted to actively pursue and bring to light the evil that surrounded Holly and her mother, she would have to be given that charge.

Ariel pursed her lips and gave her perfect little chin an upward thrust. She'd never heard of a ten-year-old Avenging Angel, but there was always a first time for anything—even in heavenly circles.

Chapter Two

Ariel floated through the closed door of the Denver Branch of Avenging Angels whose office was located in an inconspicuous, charming little house dwarfed by high-rise apartments and office buildings on Logan Street. Ariel had never been to the DBAA before, and she wasn't exactly sure how she should proceed.

A gray-haired receptionist wearing a name tag, Grace, sat behind a desk in the small outer room. The older angel looked up with bright blue eyes and a luminous smile, which faded slightly as she took in Ariel's bright pink pullover, blue jeans and long, lustrous blond hair pulled back from her face in a flopping ponytail. Certainly not the appearance of a heavenly angel who cared about impressions set by religious painters down through the ages, Grace thought, secretly lamenting the fact that no one used wings anymore nor wore flowing white gowns when given earthly assignments. She herself had to settle for a plain white tailored dress. Unfortunately, working with mortals and assuming mortal forms had a tendency to foster casual attire like that worn by this petite, girlish angel who materialized before her.

"Yes, dear?" she asked gently, aware of the young girl's hesitant and uneasy aura.

"I want to see someone about a change of assignment."

Grace pursed her lips, sensing trouble. Child angels had no business questioning heavenly authority. "What is the problem?"

"I don't want to be a Guardian anymore. I want to be an Avenger." There was a stubborn set to Ariel's bowed mouth.

"Now, dear, you know how well-defined the heavenly hierarchies are," Grace countered in a placating tone. "Your assignment as a Guardian Angel cannot be changed because you have a whim to be an Avenging Angel. All aspects of a situation are taken into consideration before an assignment is made."

"But that's the reason I need to be reassigned. The situation has changed. Terribly. Someone is trying to harm my five-year-old charge and her mother. Please, I need to talk to the Heavenly Avenging Angel in charge. Please...?"

Grace couldn't ignore the sincere pleading in the girl's voice. Convinced that something more than a whim was prompting the girl angel's request to be reassigned, she glanced at her gold-leafed appointment book. "I don't know. Angelo has a full morning." She paused. "Maybe I could squeeze you in before the general celestial meeting. I'm not promising that it will do you any good, but you can tell him your story."

"Thank you, Grace," Ariel said with proper respect.

Grace motioned Ariel to follow her through a small archway into a spacious center room. Rafters stretched across a high ceiling, and at one end of the room, French doors opened onto a small patio. A staircase mounted one wall to a balcony that over looked the main room.

Grace pointed upward toward the balcony. "Angelo's office is the first door on the right. Good luck," she said, and with a swish she was gone.

Ariel mounted the steps slowly instead of floating up them as she usually did. She felt constrained by the earthiness of her surroundings and was more conscious of the strict code governing the conduct of angels when dealing with mortals. Most of the limitations had never bothered Ariel. Lying, swearing or breaking the other Ten Commandments had never been a threat to her holy status. She'd fouled up a few times learning how to control her powers. Sometimes she gave in to girlish exuberance, riding merry-go-rounds, taking horseback rides at midnight or playing tricks on Holly's dog, Jiggs. She hoped her pranks wouldn't be held against her. Up until now, she'd been content to be a playmate, a companion and loving guardian, but the threat against Holly and her mother had changed all that. If she was to identify the evil force threatening their lives, she needed broader deductive powers and the backing of St. Michael's Avenging Angels.

As Ariel paused in front of Angelo's door, it slowly swung open by itself.

"Come in, Ariel."

As she entered the pristine white room, she felt the overwhelming warmth of the Italian angel's presence. Midnight blue eyes dominated Angelo's strong masculine features, and his thick, muscular body seemed out of place in the confines of an office as he leaned back in his massive chair. His craggy face softened by a luminous light as he said, "Please, sit down."

He motioned to a chair that was much too large for her petite frame, but she did as she was told. She perched on the edge of the seat and her feet didn't touch the floor even when she sat straight without touching the back of the chair.

Angelo's booming voice softened. "I heard what you said to Grace." He put the tips of his large fingers together in a waiting gesture. "You want a change in assignment, is that correct, Ariel?"

She met his eyes squarely. "I want to be an Avenging Angel."

"I see. And you know all about this select order of angels?"

"I know that they are the angels that fight against injustice. In the Bible they swept down from heaven with a vengeance, and sometimes they even used flaming swords to right a wrong."

A smile quivered at the corner of Angelo's broad lips. "Is that what this is about, Ariel? You'd like to have a flaming sword?"

Her slender nose wrinkled slightly. "I don't think so. Would I have to have one?"

Angelo chuckled and shook his dark head. "No. Flaming swords aren't regular issue for Avenging Angels these days. Now, suppose you tell me why a little girl angel like yourself wants an assignment to fight an injustice."

Without hesitation Ariel told him about the accident and the insight of evil she'd experienced earlier. "Someone tampered with the car and left his dark aura around it," she explained solemnly. "Someone meant for the car to go off the road. Don't you see how important it is to find out who this person is and expose him?''

"And you think you can do that?'' Angelo questioned. "You know you have to work through the mortals involved. They have to come to the truth themselves and deal with the situation. Instead of only being a Guardian Angel to one little girl, you'd have to expand your sphere of influence. As well as protecting the mortals involved, you'd have to use deductive measures to find the evil one and then bring about a human awareness of that identity.''

"I could do all of that," Ariel said with a pugnacious lift of her chin.

"And what if you fail?"

Her deep blue eyes rounded as if the prospect of failure had never entered her head. "Fail?"

"Angels are neither all-knowing nor all-powerful, and our limitations make it impossible to interfere with human free will. Unfortunately, mortals are often blind to the truth, and when they stubbornly go their own way, there's nothing we can do about it. Even though your intentions in identifying this evil and bringing it to justice are the best, Ariel, I have to warn you that this kind of assignment will present new challenges on many different levels. It won't be easy. If my best avengers, Dashiell, Kiel and Samuel weren't already assigned, I wouldn't even consider your request.''

"Then you're going to let me do it?'' she said eagerly as if his consideration was as sure as a done deal.

He leaned forward and put her in his shadow. "I don't think you realize what's involved, Ariel. You can't just use angel magic to discover where the evil is coming from. It's not that easy. And in order to bring a guilty soul to justice, you'll have to work within earthly resources available. The evidence you have against the guilty one will have to stand up in court. That's the way earthly justice works. Do you understand what I'm saying?''

She nodded. ''We have to get the goods on the guy.''

Angelo laughed again. ''Exactly.''

''Then you'll let me do it,'' she repeated.

He was silent for a long moment and then nodded. ''Yes, I'm going to give you permission. But, Ariel, you have to promise to ask for help if you need it.''

''I will. I will.''

''A word of warning. Maybe you have misinterpreted the situation completely. It might not be as dire as you believe. Cars have mechanical failures all the time and you might have misread the dark energy field.''

Ariel knew better than to argue. She simply nodded and took her leave. Her conviction that Holly and her mother were the victims of evil intentions had not wavered. She had no doubt at all—someone wanted them dead.

DAYS AND NIGHTS in the hospital were a blur for Shanna as she fought the pain in her head and endured a myriad of tests. Everything about the accident floated in her memory like disjointed pieces. Losing control of the runaway car. Trees and rocks whizzing by at frantic speed. The horrible sensation of plunging over the cliff. Screams caught in her chest, perspiration beaded on her forehead, and her chilled body shivered. As if in a torturous nightmare, she lived the horror over and over again.

"It's all right. You're going to be fine." Gentle hands smoothed back the damp hair from her forehead.

She knew the voice, welcomed the familiar touch. He was only a blurred figure standing by her bed, but the warm contact flowing between them steadied Shanna just the way it had on the hillside when he had talked quietly to her during the agonizing eternity waiting for the ambulance. He'd risked his life by pulling her and Holly out of the car in time. She'd never be able to repay him for that selfless courage.

He was a constant visitor at the hospital, and his familiar, reassuring voice continued to be an anchor in a world cloaked in vague shadows and darkness. She wondered how old he was and what kind of features went with his sure, dexterous hands. She remembered the scent of the jacket he'd placed over her at the accident, and that clean, masculine scent had now become familiar to her.

His name was Dr. Jay Harrison, she knew that. And after she'd been in the hospital nearly a week, she'd learned a little bit about him from one of the nurses.

"He's from New York, spending a little time in Colorado while his dad recuperates. His father, Dr. Bradley Harrison, is a GP who just had bypass surgery. I guess he took over his dad's commitment to spend a couple of days in Westridge's mountain clinic."

"What does he look like?"

The young nurse's voice took on a dreamy air. "If Dr. Jay Harrison took off his shirt, mussed up his wavy brown hair and looked straight into a camera with those midnight blue eyes, he'd make a heck of a model for a hunk calendar."

Shanna smiled. She got the picture.

The next time he came, she said, "I've never thanked you for all you did for us, Dr. Harrison."

"Jay," he corrected her. His experienced eyes took in the pain lines on her forehead and the dark shadows on her cheeks. He'd kept himself informed of her condition and had been relieved when the tests showed that her vision had not been permanently damaged. "I hear you're going to be released in a few days."

She bit her lip. "But I still can't see anything clearly. Everything is blurred, like I'm looking through rain-spattered glass."

"The specialist says that once the fluid behind your pupils is absorbed your vision should returned to normal. You'll have to give yourself some time."

"But that's what I don't have—time. I've a child to care for, a house to get in shape and a living to make. I've already taken out a loan to make improvements on the house." She drew in a breath to steady her voice. "I'm sorry. I didn't mean to unload on you. I'll manage." Her chin came up. "I always have. My late husband was away for months at a time, and I'm used to solving problems on my own. I'll get through this somehow."

"I know you will." From the first moment he'd pulled her from the car, she had engaged his emotions with a bewildering intensity and had been constantly at the front of his thoughts. As he looked down into her swimming blue eyes a surge of sexual awareness mocked the professional bedside manner he had been trying to maintain.

There had been plenty of attractive women patients who could have fired his male hormones if he'd been the least bit interested, but he'd chosen to stay faithful to the woman he'd married—even though Valerie had turned out to be the wrong choice for a wife. Well, he'd learned his lesson. He wasn't going to let any woman, however appealing, turn his life into hell again.

Jay drew his hand away from Shanna's and said briskly, "You'll have to make some adjustments, of course, but there are lots of people with less vision than you have who function very well."

Shanna heard the withdrawal in his voice. He was pulling back, putting distance between them. Obviously, he didn't want her leaning on him. Her pride flared. "Thanks again for all your help," she said in a dismissing tone. "Holly and I will make out just fine."

"How is she?"

"Fine. A friend of my Aunt Emma's is taking care of her." Thank heavens for Ruby Thompson, thought Shanna. The older woman had brought Holly to the hospital every day to see her. The visits had been painful for Shanna because she couldn't see either of them clearly. Terror tore at her heart when she had pulled Holly to her and could only see the dark and light shadows of her child's face. She had to pretend that she wasn't worried about her eyesight coming back.

What if didn't? What if the doctors were wrong? What if the murky gray curtain obscuring her vision never rose and let her see things clearly again? Shifting shadows and washed-out light allowed only indistinct impressions of forms and empty spaces. Like a blurred negative, her vision constantly shifted in shades of gray, black and anemic colors. She couldn't judge height or depth, and even the most familiar object seemed alien, but she wasn't going to give in to her fears. She couldn't. "A few more days in the hospital and I'll be able to see well enough to go home."

Jay heard the frightened catch in her throat. Throwing caution aside, he sat down on the edge of the bed and took her hand. His throat tightened as he stiffened against the impulse to kiss away the tears welling at the corner of her eyes. He couldn't believe such desires were even crossing his mind.

She felt the warmth of his long, tapering fingers as they closed over hers. Wonderful, smooth, strong hands, she thought, just right for a doctor's.

A tingling radiated from the contact, and they sat in silence for a long charged moment. He knew he was letting his emotions get out of control, and if he'd learned anything from the fiasco of his marriage, it was to keep his professional and personal life separate. Valerie had been his patient once, and look how that had turned out.

He cleared his throat and tried to keep a betraying huskiness out of his voice. "Maybe you shouldn't be in such a hurry to go back to Westridge. Can't both of you stay with this friend for a while?"

"No. Ruby Thompson is in her seventies and lives in a tiny retirement apartment." Shanna firmed her chin. "I'll have to manage on my own."

"Maybe you should consider a small Denver apartment—"

"No. That's not an option," she said firmly. "As soon as I'm released, we'll go back to Westridge."

"At the very least, you ought to consider having someone move into the house temporarily to help you out."

She choked back a quick retort. *And where is the money going to come from to pay for that kind of care?* She wasn't about to reveal her precarious financial position, nor was she going to be dependent on anyone, paid or otherwise. She'd get through this by herself. And she'd let him know that he was under no obligation to continue his Good Samaritan role.

He saw a flicker of stubborn determination cross her face as she took her hand from his. Her inner strength and fortitude impressed him, but he was also annoyed. He made a decision—whether Shanna Ryan wanted him to or not, he was going drive her back to Westridge and get her settled in the old house as best he could.

ON THE EARLY-MORNING drive back to Westridge, Shanna had little to say and was grateful that Jay didn't try to keep up a conversation. Without being able to see the turns in the road or anticipate the rising and falling of the roadbed, she endured a sickening vertigo that kept her holding on to the seat arm. Indistinct forms kept rushing at her from every side, and the more she tried to pierce the shadowy curtain in front of her eyes, the more she realized how nearly blind she was. Her chest tightened as she tried to convince herself that she could manage the challenges that lay ahead. How could she cope with a house and a small child for even a short time?

Holly sat in the back seat happily chatting with her pretend friend, Ariel, and showing her the rag doll Ruby had given her. Jay listened to her childish play and puzzled over the appearance and disappearance of the blond-headed young girl who had led him to the accident scene. He didn't want to think about what would have happened if she hadn't flagged him down. He could have driven right past the spot where the car hung on the rocky ledge and never have known that a mother and child were trapped in it. Just thinking about the near tragedy made him send an anxious glance at Shanna. He could tell from her rigid posture and the beaded moisture on her brow that she was fighting to keep her composure. He was worried about leaving her alone in this condition, but at the moment he didn't know what he could do about it.

When they reached Westridge, he turned north on a dirt road that led up to a two-storied house built against the rising slope of a wooded hillside. Chimneys and attic dormers, gingerbread eaves and a wide porch circling the first floor lent a picturesque charm to the Victorian-style house. Jay surveyed the place as he braked to a stop at the side of the house. The exterior needed painting, and some of the window frames need replacing. The interior probably needed as much work as the outside, he thought. Yes, money would have to be spent to turn it into a profitable B and B, probably more money than Shanna realized.

"Well what do you think?" she asked as though she'd been aware of his scrutiny even if she couldn't see his expression.

"Visitors who want to experience the Old West should love staying in an old Victorian house," he hedged, and silently added, *If they have all the comforts of a Holiday Inn.*

Shanna's face lifted. "That's what I thought. There's a lot of wonderful furniture in the house and some paint and new wallpaper will..." She broke off. How would she be able to pick out colors and patterns? She couldn't.

Jay watched her expression crumple and resisted the temptation to reach out and take her hand. "Everything takes time," he cautioned, knowing that her frustrations were just beginning.

"Yes, time." *How much time?*

"Well, let's get you settled." He came around the car and helped her out, and opened the back door for Holly. The little girl bounded up the front steps and waited impatiently for her mother to hurry up and open the front door.

Jay put a guiding hand on her arm, and when they reached the front steps, she let her other hand feel for a wrought-iron banister.

LOOKING DOWN, SHANNA realized once again how distorted her vision was. The front steps blended together without depth, and the porch floor wavered in a swirl of gray mist. She was unsure where to put her feet because of her lack of depth perception. The full extent of her handicap suddenly hit her. Nothing was going to be familiar.

"Easy," Jay said as he felt a shudder ripple through her slender body and saw how undisguised anxiety pinched the lines of her sweet mouth. "Hey, you're going to do fine. Just give yourself a little time."

Time. There was that word again.

"Careful, one more step," he cautioned as she stumbled. "Where are your keys?"

"At the bottom of the ravine with my car," she said with forced lightness. "But there's an extra house key behind the porch light."

"Well, I guess that's better than under the welcome mat," he chided as he retrieved the skeleton key, "but not much better." He unlocked the door and guided her inside.

Holly raced in, but Shanna's heart lurched and she froze in the middle of the front hall, unable to move forward as an inky darkness closed in on her. She swallowed back a legion of fears and drew in a ragged breath to keep a sob trapped in her throat. This was her house, but she realized now that she had been plunged into a dangerously alien world.

Holly bounced past her and ran down the hall to the back of the house, calling, "Jiggs! Jiggs!"

Jay had arranged for Aunt Emma's former handyman to take care of the dog while Shanna was in the hospital. She could hear the dog's excited barking and Holly's joyful squeals, but instead of moving toward the commotion, she just stood motionless inside the door. Outside in the light of day, sunlight had made it possible for her to have a vague impression of light and dark shapes, but in the dim interior of the house that distinction was gone. She couldn't make herself move forward into the dark cavern that lay before her.

Jay turned on a hall light and resisted the temptation to put his arm around her waist and lead her through the house. "Is that any better?"

"Not much."

"Put your arms out in front and slowly walk forward," he ordered. "The newel post on the staircase is lined up with the front door. Take about five steps forward."

She hesitated, not trusting the engulfing shadows that surrounded her like a moonless night in dark woods. Her heart lodged in her throat and she swallowed hard.

"There's nothing between you and the staircase," he reassured her.

She put her hands out as he had instructed and tentatively took a step forward.

"One . . . two . . . three," he counted as she moved forward. "Only two more steps . . . that's it!"

A wave of relief crossed her face as her searching hands found the old-fashioned carved newel post. She let out the breath she'd been holding.

"Good job," Jay said as he moved to her side. A rapid breathing was faintly visible in the rise and fall of her full breasts. He let his fingers linger for a moment on the soft curve of her shoulder. He was surprised when she leaned into him with a gasp of relief as if she'd been lost and had suddenly found her way. He wanted to cup her pale face with his hands and lower his mouth to hers and still the trembling of her lips.

Watch it, an inner voice ordered. He knew he was dangerously close to losing a detached perspective when it came to Shanna Ryan. He searched her face as if the answer for the sexual attraction lay in the delicate curl of her eyelashes and the delicate softness of her face. If he didn't guard against it, his involvement in her life could turn into an intimacy that would be a disaster for both of them.

He dropped his hands. "Are you all right now?"

She nodded.

"Good. Now, if you let your hand trail along the wall and walk toward the back of the house, you can make your way directly to the kitchen."

His brisk and professional tone wasn't lost on her. She cursed the momentary weakness that had made her lean into his strong, muscular body. He was just trying to help her cope, nothing more. She'd never been a clinging, helpless female, and she wasn't going to turn into one now. Embarrassment brought heat up into her face. Even though fear curled in her chest, she started forward into the depths of the dark tunnel.

"That's it. Just let your hand trail along the hall wall to guide you. Pretty soon you'll get a good feeling about distance."

As she drew closer to the kitchen she could make out a patch of light that was the door into the large room. She halted in the doorway and tried to get her bearings. With bright sunlight pouring in through the back window, the room was not in inky shadows like the front hall. She could make out vague shapes that she identified in her mind as table, chairs, cupboards and appliances.

She knew Jay was watching her as she felt her way around the room from counter to counter. The challenges facing her almost overwhelmed her determination to handle things on her own. How would she ever find anything in the cupboards? Turn on the electric burners to the correct heat? Prepare and serve food? She swallowed against the rising dryness in her throat.

The hillside outside the window remained a blur as she desperately squinted and tried to bring it into focus. She could hear Holly outside playing with the dog, but she couldn't see them through the murky haze of the glass pane. She could face her limitations better if only she knew how long it would be before her vision cleared. And what if it didn't? No, she mustn't think along those lines. Nothing was going to happen to keep her in this state of near-blindness. She just had to be patient and let time have a chance to do its healing. She turned away from the window. "It's going to be more difficult than I thought."

Jay realized that he'd have to take charge of the situation whether he wanted to or not. She needed someone to look out for her welfare.

"I want you and Holly to move into my father's cabin instead of staying here," he said in a firm, no-argument tone. "The place is small, modern and much easier for you to manage."

"No, I couldn't. I—"

"Don't argue. I've only been using the place overnight a couple of times a week. It has two bedrooms. You and Holly can use one and I'll use the other when I'm around. And I could help with the cooking. Even give you a hand with Holly and other things." He couldn't believe he was putting himself in this kind of situation, but damn it, she was alone, and had a kid to look after and an old house that needed plenty of work. What a laugh his New York friends would have if they knew he was proposing to play house with some gal. He was surprised at himself. "You're going to need my help."

Shanna heard pity in his tone. He didn't think she could manage by herself. He was going to take charge and tell her what to do. Even though a part of her cried out for some strong arm to lean on, she'd learned in the past that the only true support came from within herself. She wasn't about to turn over the control of her life to someone else. She was already obligated to him more than she would have liked. "I appreciate the offer, but I couldn't."

"Why not?" He smarted at her blunt refusal. He wasn't in the habit of involving himself in other people's misfortune, and he wasn't prepared for a flat refusal when he offered help.

"I want to stay here."

"Don't be foolish. There's no sense in your staying here, trying to handle this all by yourself."

"This is my home. I don't want to live somewhere else." She knew that her stiff-necked pride was showing, but she couldn't help it. His authoritative tone only strengthened her resolve not to be dependent on this stranger. She knew him only by voice and touch. This was her battle, and no one could fight it for her. "Thanks again for your help, but I can manage fine."

He swore under his breath. She stood there so damn vulnerable that he wanted to jerk her into his arms and kiss away her blasted pride. He'd never had a woman challenge him on so many levels. From the moment he'd seen her slumped over the steering wheel, he'd spent hours thinking about her and worrying about the prognosis of her condition. He didn't understand his feelings for her, but one thing he did understand—her pointed rejection of his offer to take care of her made him look like a sentimental fool.

"All right. If that's your decision. I brought along a box of stick-on dots to mark the stove knobs, the water faucets, all the canned goods, and anything else that needs identification," he said. "You'll be able to tell from the number of dots, like braille, exactly what's what by touch."

"I hadn't even thought about doing something like that!"

"And here's something to help you know what time it is." He put a rectangular object in her hands and moved a finger to push down on a small knob.

"Eight-thirteen a.m.," advised a mechanical voice.

A small smile played at the corner of her mouth. The talking clock and Jay's thoughtfulness steadied her. It was going to be all right. If people who were blind from birth could manage, she could certainly cope for a short time with limited vision.

He saw her shoulders straighten. No use trying to fight a losing battle, he thought. She'd made her decision and she wasn't going to give an inch. "Have you decided which rooms you want to rearrange?"

"Luckily there's a first-floor bedroom that Aunt Emma used in her later years. I'll move into it. The small connecting sitting room has a day couch that would serve nicely as Holly's bed."

"Bathroom?"

"There's a small downstairs bathroom next to the kitchen." Her spirits rose as she spoke. The kitchen, bedroom, sitting room and bath would serve as a small apartment, and once she became familiar with the way everything was arranged, she ought to be able to move around easily.

Jay looked over the bedroom and sitting room.

"What do you think?" Shanna asked anxiously.

"If we rearrange a few things, I think these rooms should work out fine."

Without waiting for her approval, he moved beds, chairs, small tables, a sofa, dresser and bookcase, trying to eliminate as many trouble spots as possible. "I'm putting the big easy chair close to the bed and moving your aunt's little table, footstool and lamp out of the middle of the floor. That way, the floor will be clear between your room and the sitting room where Holly would be sleeping."

She nodded in agreement.

"You'll get familiar with everything very quickly," he assured her. "Come on, I'll give you a guided tour," he said when he'd finished, and took her arm.

She tried to imprint a picture of the two rooms in her mind as he led her around them several times in an effort to orient her to the furniture arrangement. She hadn't paid particular attention to the former furniture arrangement during her short stay in the house, so had no memory to rely upon. But maybe that was better, she tried to tell herself.

When Jay took away his guiding hand, he urged her to walk around the rooms by herself. Several times she stopped in the middle of the floor, suddenly terrified to take a step forward. The lack of depth perception gave the impression of vacant air beneath her feet. She choked back a surge of panic, feeling like someone poised on a diving board with no assurance of water in the pool beneath her.

Jay moved closer but did not touch her or offer help. She could feel his warm breath bathing her cheek, and that familiar masculine scent brought back her courage. She stepped boldly forward, her hand outstretched until she touched a doorframe and walked into the sitting room and across the rug to Holly's couch bed.

Jay clapped his hands. "Bravo. You're doing fine. I'll ask the clinic nurse to come over today and bring down your things from the bedrooms and bathroom. Marla's a good soul. She'll be glad to help out."

The idea of a complete stranger going through her things made Shanna feel uncomfortable, but she held her tongue. This was no time for false pride. She'd have to accept the other woman's help and be glad for it.

"And remember, my offer stands. If things don't work out and you change your mind about staying here, let me know."

"I will," she promised, but there was little indication in her firm voice that she would even consider changing her mind.

"Well, I'm due at the clinic in fifteen minutes. Is there anything else I can do before I leave?"

Shanna shook her head. "I'll walk you to the door."

Jay was glad she couldn't see his look of surprise nor his admiring grin as she put her hand out, moved forward and touched the wide molding of the hall doorframe.

"Good girl," he murmured. He had promised himself that he'd do what he could to get her settled in the house and then distance himself from any personal involvement, but he knew that such detachment was going to be more difficult than he had expected. He walked beside her without touching her as she let her hand trail along the wall until they reached the front hall.

Faint gray impressions of two narrow windows on each side of the front door guided Shanna forward across the front hall. When she reached out and touched the doorknob, a smile of victory curved her lips. "I guess you can find your way from here."

He laughed at her impudent sarcasm. "I'll know who to call if I get lost."

"Jay, I...I don't want you to think I don't appreciate what you've done," she stammered. "It's just...it's just..."

"Just that you have to do everything the hard way," he finished.

"No, just *my* way," she corrected him.

"You have the most stubborn, willful and delightful chin I've ever seen," he said, tipping it up with one finger and lightly placing a kiss on her hairline. He could have added that she had the kind of tempting, kissable mouth that could drive any man crazy. "I'll check on you tonight before I go to the cabin."

"You don't have to do that."

"All right, I won't if you don't want me to." He waited.

She swallowed. "I guess I want you to."

He gave a satisfied chuckle. "I thought you might."

She felt his eyes locking with hers, and impulsively she reached out and let her fingers trace the firm lines and planes of cheek, chin and mouth. A tension like an electric wire snapped inside her. For a fleeting moment she reacted to a charged heat radiating between them, and she knew she wanted him to kiss her.

He saw the willing lift of her head and tantalizing parting of her soft lips. Heat flared within him, and he wanted to claim her mouth with his and press her sweet length against every inch of his body. He suppressed a groan. No, he couldn't do it. She was too vulnerable now. A momentary pleasure could turn into disaster for both of them. As much as he wanted to give in to the overwhelming need to kiss and caress her, he stepped back.

"Call me at the clinic if you need me." He gave her the number and quickly went out the door.

She listened to his footsteps retreating down the front steps and again she was furious with herself for behaving the way she had. Touching his face. Lifting her face to his. She berated herself for the weakness that had insulted him—and her. It was common knowledge that a doctor was always at the mercy of women patients who wanted more than just professional attention. Jay must be sidestepping come-ons all the time. How could she have so humiliated herself? Never in her life had she felt the way she did now. More than her eyes must need healing, she thought ironically.

She drew in a shaky breath, turned around and let her hand trail along the wall as she made her way to the kitchen. *All right. Let's get this show on the road.* She made her way to the back door and called Holly.

The little girl came bounding in with Jiggs. "We were playing hide the stick with Ariel."

"That's nice, sweetheart. Come, I want to show you the nice new room you're going to have for a while."

As Holly accompanied her mother into the sitting room, Ariel decided that it was probably time to turn her attention from being a Guardian to being a sleuth.

Where should I start?

Was there something in the house that might offer a clue to the diabolical person who had sabotaged the car? Not knowing what she was looking for, Ariel made a flying tour of the house from top to bottom. Like a whirlwind, she swished about the attic and closed-off rooms on the second floor, lifting dust-covers on the furniture, sailing under beds and invading large walk-in closets filled with old clothes smelling of mothballs.

The two upstairs bedrooms Shanna had previously chosen for herself and Holly were still littered with boxes and unpacked belongings, but Ariel sensed nothing in the moving clutter that was cause for concern. Every room was filled with Aunt Emma's furniture and belongings, and Ariel picked up the lingering aura of the woman who had loved them.

There were no dark harbingers of evil in the house, so the threat to Shanna must not have extended to her aunt. When Ariel had searched every corner of the house to her satisfaction, she floated through one of the windows and perched on the slanted roof outside.

Below the house, a cluster of buildings on Main Street showed through a canopy of tree branches, and Ariel could see scattered homes and ranches stretched in both directions along the narrow valley. The setting was idyllic, but Ariel tuned out the lilting call of a blue jay and ignored the bright eyes of a brown squirrel twisting his tail in a nearby tree.

What now? She'd found no hint of evil in the house. Her telepathic awareness had failed to pick up any hint of the dark aura that had been around the car. This sleuthing business wasn't going to be as easy as she'd hoped.

Someone must have arranged the near-fatal accident. But why? The usual reasons—money, property, jealousy and revenge—didn't seem to apply. Shanna didn't have any money in the bank, investments, stocks, or any of those other assets that mortal grown-ups worried about.

Property? Did someone want the old house badly enough to kill for it? That didn't make sense because Shanna's death wouldn't drop it in anybody's lap. But then, murder never made sense, Ariel thought wearily. Humans never seemed to realize how trivial were most of the things they organized their lives around.

Ariel contemplated jealousy and revenge. Knowing Shanna's life the way she did, such motives were out of the question. There hadn't been any other men in Shanna's life before or after her husband's death. She'd had always ignored the flirtatious advances and appreciative glances that had come her way when she'd been living on army bases. She'd been a faithful wife and loving mother, and Ariel knew that Shanna hadn't harmed anyone. Still, someone hated her enough to make certain she lost control of her car. Someone hated her enough to want her dead. And what was scary was that neither Dr. Jay nor Shanna realized it.

That brought up the next problem. Angelo had warned her that the dispensing of earthly justice couldn't be done by angel magic. Getting the goods on someone and making a case against them depended upon human effort. All right, that should be easy enough. All she needed was a buddy in the sleuthing business. Someone who had a personal investment in protecting Shanna. Someone who would be receptive to following up leads. A human partner who could put whatever evidence came to light into the hands of the proper authorities. Ariel smiled smugly. It didn't take magical angel wisdom to figure that one out. Jay Harrison was made to order.

An hour later, Shanna had just finished wiping off the kitchen counters and table, pleased with herself for handling the hot and cold water without difficulty, and was just in the process of trying to decide what she should do next when she was startled by a loud knocking on the back door. Who could that be?

Trying to get her bearings, she reached out and touched the back of a kitchen chair and took several hesitant steps toward the door. Should she tell them to come in before she knew who it was? Was the back door locked?

Jiggs bounded into the kitchen, barking and making such a fuss that her voice couldn't have been heard above the bedlam even if she'd been shouting. Holly ran in from the sitting room, where she'd been playing with her Barbie doll. "Who is it, Mama?"

"I don't know. Quiet, Jiggs! Quiet. Stop that barking!"

Holly peered through the door glass. "It's a man in a baseball hat." Without waiting for her mother's instructions, Holly turned the lock and opened the door. Instantly Jiggs's barking changed to enthusiastic leaps of joy.

"Hello, boy. How ya doing? Glad to have yer folks back, I bet. I came by just to make sure."

"Oh, you must be the kind neighbor who's been looking after Jiggs," said Shanna, remembering that Jay had asked Aunt Emma's handyman to look after the dog while she was in the hospital.

"Yes, ma'am. I hear ya had a bit of trouble with your car. Went off the road, did it? Lots of folks take them curves too fast. You were lucky. Just got eye trouble, I hear."

No need for the Internet in this town, Shanna thought. "Please come in, Mr. . . . ?"

"Lewis Walker. Just call me, Lew. Me and Emma never stood much on formalities."

His voice was not youthful but not old, either, Shanna thought, frustrated by the inability to see him. "I'm glad to meet you. I know you were a big help to my aunt."

"Emma was a grand old gal. I'm going to miss her." There was no doubt about the sincerity in his voice.

"Won't you have a seat? Can I get you something to drink?"

"I'll take a Coke," Holly piped up eagerly as if the invitation included her.

Shanna laughed. "All right, honey. Get a can out of the fridge."

Holly darted back into the sitting room with her drink, and Ariel was pulled in two directions. As a Guardian Angel she would have stayed at Holly's side, and kept a protective vigil over the child, but her new assignment made other demands. She was feeling the heavy responsibility of evaluating everyone and everything that touched the family. Her decision made, she perched unseen on a kitchen counter and prepared to analyze everything the lanky, long-haired fellow in worn jeans had to say.

"Would you like coffee or a soft drink?" Shanna asked.

"No, thanks," Lew said, "but I'll just sit a spell."

"Please do."

He waited until she had eased down into a kitchen chair and then he pulled out one for himself. She suspected that he had spent a lot of hours in this kitchen, and as if to verify her thoughts, he said, "We were good friends, your aunt and me."

"I'm glad," Shanna said sincerely.

"I helped keep this place up. More than five years I've been doing odd jobs for her. Never knew she had any close kin. Kind of a surprise to learn she left the property to a niece who never came around. You being her only living relative, and all."

Shanna decided to ignore the edge of criticism in his tone. She felt badly enough that she'd never made the effort to come back for a visit during her marriage. Coping with her wayward husband, the constant upheaval of moving, and raising Holly in a disintegrating marriage had taken precedent over a trip to see Aunt Emma. Shanna still felt a pang of guilt over inheriting her aunt's property, but she was determined to use the inheritance to make a future for herself and Holly.

"I'm going to be needing some work done, Lew. Would you be interested in doing some odd jobs for me?" Shanna quickly explained her intent to start a bed-and-breakfast business. She couldn't tell from his shifting feet whether or not he was comfortable with the idea.

"I don't think Emma would hold with a lot of strangers tramping in and out of her house."

"It's my house now," Shanna said with more emphasis that she had intended.

"So it is," he said shortly. "But I'm thinking you may decide to turn the property into a bit of cash and move someplace else."

"I don't think so," she answered flatly. "I've made up my mind to stay in Westridge."

"Well, now, I wouldn't be biting off more than you can chew right now, with your eyes and all."

"My condition is only temporary. In a few weeks my eyes will be back to normal." *Please, Lord, make it so,* she prayed.

"Well, I guess we can wait until then to talk about work. Anybody going to be staying with you?"

She didn't want it broadcast around town that she was alone, so she avoided answering and said instead, "Thanks again for looking after Jiggs."

"I'll be stopping by…in case you need anything. Kinda got the habit of spending my evenings with Emma. She invited me to move in with her more than once, but said there was too much age difference for us to be marrying. I always thought…" His voice grew strident. "Well, no matter. The place is yours now."

"Tell me about Westridge," Shanna invited as a silence fell.

"Not much to tell. We're kinda off the beaten track. The closest ski resort is eighteen miles away. Thank God for that. A few summer homes bring in a few more people, but the year-round population stays pretty much the same."

"I'm surprised that more people haven't moved in. I mean, it's not far from Denver, and it has beautiful scenery and plenty of places to camp. I would have thought that there'd be plenty of visitors, especially in the summer."

"Have you met the Rendells?"

"Janet Rendell paid me a visit. And Billie Jo."

"Texans," he said as if that was identification enough.

Shanna suppressed a smile. Apparently the welcome mat wasn't out for outsiders moving into the state, especially Texans. Having lived on army bases, she'd always found natives of the Lone Star state to be friendly sorts. At the same time, she wasn't at all sure that Janet fit into that positive category. Her friendliness seemed quite calculated. Knowing she was deliberately encouraging Lew to gossip, Shanna said, "Mrs. Rendell told me she writes a column for the weekly paper."

"So I hear. Don't read the local rag myself. I get all the news I want down at the Timberline Bar. The locals keep up on what's going on without some outsider trying to tell them what's what."

"The Rendells aren't considered local?"

"Naw. They bought some fishing cabins along the creek a couple of years ago. Rent 'em out to a bunch of their beer-drinking cronies. Emma and me used to sit on the porch and listen to their carousing. I'd give 'em a wide berth if I was you. They was always pestering Emma about selling this place to them.''

"Really?"

"Yep."

Shanna remembered the way Janet had been constantly looking around. "I'm surprised. She didn't have anything good to say about the house, and she acted as if she hadn't been in it before."

"Probably just sizing up the place. Emma gave them short shift when they came calling. She wasn't interested in any of their big talking. I'm a-thinkin' she wouldn't have sold to them if the property *had* been for sale."

"But why would they want this old house?"

"They had some idea of adding on to it. Making it into some darn fool fishing lodge so more of their Texas cronies would have a place to stay," he snorted. "Your aunt told them to hike up their boots and git. Emma wasn't turning over her house to the likes of them, no sirree." The timbre of his voice changed, and she knew he was glaring at her. "They'll probably be at you to sell the place."

"She didn't say anything about being interested in the property. But she wasn't very encouraging when I told her about my plans for a B and B."

"I think it's a dumb fool idea myself." Lew got to his feet.

Shanna set her chin. "I have to support myself and my child, and I think that Aunt Emma would approve."

"How well did you know her?"

"Not very well," Shanna admitted.

"Then don't say I didn't warn you about turning her home into a tourist trap." With that he marched out of the house and let the door bang loudly behind him.

Chapter Three

When Jay walked into the clinic, Marla greeted him with eyes snapping with curiosity. "We've been hearing all kinds of exciting things about your daring rescue, Dr. Jay. What on earth happened? Did you see the woman's car go off the road?"

Jay reached for his white coat. "No, it happened a few minutes before I reached that spot. A little girl saw the car go over the embankment. I don't know who she is. Probably lives in one of those homes scattered all over the hillside. Anyway, she flagged me down and showed me the place." Jay felt his stomach tighten just remembering the scene. "The car was caught on a ledge and hung there long enough for me to get Shanna and Holly out."

"How badly were they hurt?"

"Miraculously the child escaped without a scratch. Shanna…Mrs. Ryan…suffered a head injury that has affected her eyes. Her vision should clear as the fluid behind the retina is absorbed. But at the moment, she has an impression of dark and light and that's about all." Jay turned away so Marla wouldn't see the concern he knew must be in his eyes. He'd never been much good at pretense, and he didn't want the perceptive nurse to know how much his personal feelings were already involved. As casually as he could, he suggested, "Maybe, you might find time to help her, Marla. She'd probably appreciate a woman's touch in moving her personal things downstairs."

"Sure, I'll run by on my noon break and say hello."

"Thanks. Now, what's on the schedule today?" Determinedly, he put aside a lingering uneasiness and concentrated on a parade of patients with minor ailments.

SHANNA MADE IT THROUGH the morning without incident, but everything took twice as long. Fixing lunch was a trial as she tried to cope with her hungry daughter's impatience.

"I don't want peas, Mama. I want SpaghettiOs. You opened the wrong can," Holly wailed.

Ariel slipped into a chair next to Holly and materialized for her. "Don't give your mother a bad time," Ariel scolded like an older sister. This was no time for one of Holly's childish tantrums. Thank heavens, she usually had a sunny disposition, but when Holly's stomach was empty she could be as testy as a bear.

"I don't like peas," she whined.

"I know you're hungry, honey," Shanna answered. "But you're going to have to be patient."

Ariel nodded. Holly pursed out her lips and frowned, but she stopped her whining.

Fixing lunch in a strange kitchen without being able to see had Shanna's stomach in a tight knot. She'd never be able to remember how Jay had organized the cupboards for her. "Which can has the picture of SpaghettiOs on it?"

"That one."

"I can't see you pointing," Shanna said with forced patience. "Come here and get it off the shelf for me."

"Okay." Holly hopped down from her chair.

Ariel smiled and nodded her approval. "That's a big girl."

Holly pulled a chair over to the counter and climbed up on it. She took down the right can and handed it to Shanna. "Here, Mommy."

"Thanks, honey. You're going to be a big help," Shanna praised her as she opened the can and emptied the contents into a pan. She had just turned on the correct burner when the doorbell chimed. Jiggs gave a woof and scrambled down the hall as the front door opened.

A cheery voice floated down the hall. "Hello, Mrs. Ryan? Can I come in? I'm Dr. Jay's nurse."

Shanna smothered a groan. She remembered that Jay had said he was going to ask the nurse to come by and help move things downstairs, but she hadn't expected her so soon. She wasn't ready to parade her helplessness in front of other people. Things were moving too fast.

"We're in the kitchen." Shanna tried to put a welcoming lilt in her voice. "Come on back."

Jay had probably used his position to engage the woman's help. I should be grateful for the help, she told herself, but deep down she hated to be dependent upon anyone, especially a stranger.

Jiggs quit his welcoming bark, and Shanna heard the bouncy steps of soft-soled shoes and the slight whisper of a starched uniform as the woman and dog came into the kitchen.

"Hi, I'm Marla Dillard. Dr. Jay asked me to drop by." She had a pleasant voice with a confident, no-nonsense sound to it.

Shanna's smile wavered as she said self-consciously, "Thank you for coming. I'm Shanna, and this is my daughter, Holly."

The nurse was only a blur of white against the dark tunnel of the hall, and Shanna couldn't tell if the woman was short, tall, thin or fat but the timbre of her voice suggested someone in her middle years.

"The doctor thought you might need an extra pair of hands getting settled in."

"I'm afraid I do. Most of our things are in the upstairs bedrooms. We just moved in, you know, and we're not really settled in yet. Now that my eyesight..." Shanna's voice trailed off. She didn't know how to state the problem without seeming to dwell on her handicap.

"I can imagine how insecure you must feel trying to cope in a strange, rambling house like this." Shanna had the feeling that Marla was surveying the kitchen from top to bottom.

The kitchen was probably a total mess, thought Shanna with a spurt of irritation. A lot of her kitchenware was still in boxes to be unpacked, and as yet she hadn't given the place a good scrubbing. She'd always prided herself on being an immaculate housekeeper and, if anything, had faulted on the side of being too much of a perfectionist. She despaired to think of anyone seeing the house before she could put it to rights.

"Do you know how to fix SpaghettiOs?" Holly piped up in the momentary silence.

Shanna's laugh was rather weak. "I think my daughter is afraid she's going to have to eat all my mistakes."

"Mama opened the wrong can. She can't see anything," Holly offered as a way of explanation.

"That's not true, Holly," Shanna corrected her daughter. She certainly wasn't about to play on this woman's sympathy. "My vision is cloudy, but that's all. And the condition isn't permanent. My eyes should be getting back to normal very shortly."

"Whatever is on the stove is about to burn," Marla said as she moved quickly across the room.

Marla put a firm hand on Shanna's arm. "Sit down," she ordered. "I really don't mind helping. I'll dish up a couple of plates."

Shanna had intended to fix a sandwich for herself, but she didn't say anything. Marla's take-charge manner was typical of the nurses she'd known both when Holly was born and her recent stay in Denver General. Giving orders was part of their job description. *Go with the flow,* she told herself. At the moment, she had neither the energy nor inclination to tell the woman that she didn't want to eat canned spaghetti. She just sat down obediently. Given the situation, she wasn't in any position to turn away any good deeds that came her way. She tried to smile as Marla's shadowy figure placed steamy plates on the table in front of her and Holly.

"It's too hot," wailed Holly.

"Blow on it," her mother prompted shortly. Shanna's stomach was too tight for any appetite. As she looked down at the table, her lack of depth perception distorted everything. She had no idea how in the world she was going to get the slippery spaghetti onto the prongs of a fork. Marla set a glass of milk on the table and guided Shanna's hand to it.

"Thank you," Shanna said as she lifted the glass and took a deep drink. When she set it down, she made a mental note as to where she had placed it, praying that she wouldn't embarrass herself by knocking it over the next time she moved her hand.

"Dr. Jay was very encouraging about your prognosis," Marla said briskly as if she empathized with Shanna's frustration. "And I could tell that he was concerned about your situation...staying in this big house and all."

"He's been very supportive," Shanna said evenly.

"Maybe he's finally found something in Westridge that interests him."

Shanna felt heat rising up in her cheeks. "He saved our lives, but there's no reason for him to continue to feel responsible for us."

"Well, it would be good news if he decided to stay in Colorado." Marla sighed. "Sure would make his father happy, but Dr. Jay's one of those diehard New Yorkers, you know. He's already getting restless, and as soon as his father has recovered from his operation, he says he'll be on a jet back to the Big Apple."

Shanna stiffened against a stab of loss that shot through her. He might return to New York any day. And why not? That's where his life was. His career. He could leave even before she had a chance to see what he looked like or even show him what she was like as her own person and not someone dependent upon his professional concerns. She despaired to think that he had seen her only at her worst.

"Don't understand how anyone could prefer pollution, noise and people living on top of one another to the clean, open spaces of the Rocky Mountains. I came here four years ago to work in the clinic, and I wouldn't live anywhere else.''

"It's going to be an adjustment for Holly and me but I think we're going to feel the same way. Dr. Jay can have his big-city life," Shanna said with a toss of her hair.

"I hate to think about breaking in another doctor if Bradley, Dr. Harrison, senior, that is, doesn't come back," confessed Marla. "We get along so well."

"Does his son resemble him?" Shanna asked, giving in to the temptation to satisfy her curiosity a little more about the man who could send her pulses racing with a touch and a word.

"Well now, I hadn't thought much about it," Marla mused. "Bradley Harrison has a broader face and slightly heavier bone structure. I'd say they're both good-looking enough. Maybe too good-looking."

There was a wistful edge to her words, and Shanna wondered if the nurse might have some romantic leanings toward the senior Dr. Harrison.

"Anyway, Dr. Jay's recently divorced, you know," Marla continued. "I can't see him getting seriously involved with anyone even under these circumstances." She paused and then said in her usual brisk manner, "I wouldn't set my sights on him if I were you."

Shanna bristled. "I assure you, I have no intention of 'setting my sights' on him or anyone else. I was just trying to gain a mental picture of him."

"Well now, if you just imagine Hugh Grant's dark eyes and tousled wavy hair and Kevin Costner's wistful smile, you'll have a pretty good likeness."

She knew Marla was watching her expression, so she just shrugged as if she couldn't care less. One thing was sure, women of all ages seemed to agree that he was terribly handsome. The young hospital nurse had described him as a calendar hunk. Undoubtably he was used to fighting off women who responded to his devastating bedside manner, thought Shanna with a touch of bitterness. She quickly turned the conversation in a different direction. "Marla, did you know my Aunt Emma?"

"Not well. Your aunt was healthy enough not to need any emergency medical attention. At least, she never came to the clinic, and she stayed pretty much to herself. She depended a lot on Lew Walker. Everybody was guessing that she'd leave this run-down old place to him."

Shanna could tell from Marla's tone that she didn't think much of the old Victorian house. Trying not to get defensive, Shanna answered evenly, "I'm planning to rent out some of the bedrooms as a bed-and-breakfast. But I won't be able to do much about getting the place ready for a while, until I get my vision back. I need to be able to supervise the work."

"Going to take a mint of money to fix it up, I'm thinking."

"Yes," Shanna admitted. Obviously the practical nurse thought she was making a big mistake. "But I'm confident I can make a go of it once I get it into shape and open for business."

"Well, good luck. I guess it wouldn't hurt the town to have a nice place for folks to stay when they pass through. Now, I'll run upstairs. Jay said you were using the downstairs bedroom and sitting room. I'll bring down some things for your immediate needs, and then I'll come back this evening to finish up."

"Everything's a mess up there. I've hung up a few clothes and put out some bathroom stuff. Holly got some of her toys out. That's about it. I really haven't unpacked.

"We can take care of some of that later."

"I don't want to impose," Shanna protested.

"It's no imposition," Marla answered briskly, and she surprised Shanna by putting her arm around Shanna's shoulder and giving her a squeeze. "We all need help from time to time."

"I've never been gracious about letting other people do things for me."

"I can see that you're a woman who wants to fight her own battles."

"Yes, I do," Shanna asserted, but there was an emptiness in her heart that mocked the truth of her words.

Shanna sat there, blinking back a sudden swell of hot tears and feeling totally inadequate and vulnerable as Marla made several trips up and down the steps. Maybe she should throw in the towel and move out of the house.

And go where?

She didn't have enough income for Holly and herself to live somewhere else. There were no relatives that would take them in. With her limited finances, hiring a housekeeper was out of the question. And she certainly wouldn't impose on Jay's hospitality. Even though he had suggested that she move into his father's cabin, she knew he must feel trapped in the situation. No, she had no choice but to manage as best she could and pray that her eyesight would quickly return to normal.

After Marla had left with the promise of returning later in the day, Shanna put Holly down for her nap in the big old-fashioned bed that had been her aunt's.

"Read to me, Mama," Holly begged, pushing a book into her mother's hands.

From the feel of its worn cover and size, Shanna guessed it was an old favorite, *The Gingerbread Man*. Luckily she knew the story by heart and turned each page as if she were reading. Holly's eyes were heavy with sleep when she'd finished, and Shanna curled up beside her and gave into the emotional and physical weariness of her own body.

Ariel smiled at the tender picture. Sometimes she wished that she could exchange places with Holly just long enough to experience the warmth of a mother's arms around her and to revel in the beauty of human love. Few mortals realized the wondrous experiences that pure love offered them, she thought regretfully as she left the room.

A good time to check out my partner.

Ariel flashed instantly to a small stone building located on Main Street next to the Timberline Bar. The two-bed clinic with a small waiting room, and an even smaller examination room, took up the front half of the building, and living quarters for a resident doctor or nurse were located in the back.

Jay was busy tending to a wiggling two-year-old boy when Ariel silently swished into the examination room. A young mother stood by anxiously as Jay stitched up the cut on the toddler's forehead. He teased the mother about having a football player in the making and managed to bring a weak smile to her lips.

Ariel watched the quick, efficient and even graceful movement of Jay's hands as he closed the wound. He offered the little boy a sucker, and Ariel took one for herself with such lightning speed that he missed what had happened.

Angels didn't need to eat, but she liked the idea of licking a gooey red sucker. And, of course, there was Holly, who was always ready to enjoy any extra sweet that came her way.

The waiting room was always full, and as Ariel watched a variety of patients come and go, she decided that Marla was a good nurse and Dr. Jay was a very skilled physician. He had a good bedside manner and listened carefully to what people had to say. But would he make a good partner when it came to acting on intuitive feelings? Would he be receptive to listening to a voice deep inside his head?

Ariel wished she could know for sure. Human beings were terribly unpredictable. If he closed his mind to the presence of a helpful spirit, the chance that they could work together would be lost.

She sighed. Only time would tell whether or not they could help each other expose the evil that threatened Shanna.

And maybe time was the one thing they didn't have.

Chapter Four

That evening Jay came back to the house with Marla, and the two of them reorganized everything on the ground floor that might give Shanna difficulty. She was a little annoyed the way the two of them talked over her head as if she were one of their patients.

"What if she needs the phone in a hurry?"

"The only one is in the hall."

"We'll have to order another extension. She should have one by her bed."

"Mark the medicine bottles. We don't want her taking aspirin or any other blood thinner."

Shanna reeled under the barrage of instructions and warnings. "Watch out." "Don't try..." "Double check." "Call for help."

Their voices reverberated in her head and knotted the tense muscles in her back and neck. An undercurrent of skepticism in their tone that she would be able to cope successfully in the situation did little to bolster her sinking confidence. A sickening tension settled in the pit of her stomach as she tried to visualize in her mind exactly where they were putting everything.

"Well, I guess that's all you'll need right away," said Marla as she finished hanging clothes in the downstairs bedroom closet. "Blue jeans, tops and sweaters are on the right. Pant suits and matching outfits are on the left. I've identified the ones that go together with safety pins. You can feel the number of pins and match them up. That way you won't have to worry about putting the wrong set together."

That's the least of my worries, Shanna thought. She hadn't even thought about her lack of color discrimination in picking out the right things to wear. She faced challenges that made her appearance of little consequence. Jeans and pullovers were her favorites, anyway, and she felt her slender figure wore them well. Still, she appreciated the nurse's efforts. "Thanks, Marla."

"I've put panties and bras in one drawer, socks and hosiery in another, slips, teddies and camisoles in another. If you don't like the arrangement, just let me know and I'll rearrange the drawers."

"No, I'm sure they'll be fine." Shanna's voice caught and she turned away, hoping that the nurse wouldn't see how devastating it was to have a perfect stranger handling her most intimate apparel. She'd never felt so exposed in her whole life. Her scanty lingerie must have brought a surprised look on Marla's face. From time to time, Shanna had ordered utterly feminine bras, bikini panties and sheer nighties from mail-order catalogs. The attempts to put some romantic fire back into her marriage had failed, and the sexy items had remained for the most part unworn in her scented drawers.

"Oh, I found these books on one of the beds upstairs. Thought I should bring them down."

"What are they?" asked Shanna, puzzled. She hadn't unpacked any of her books yet.

"A couple of school texts. Industrial arts and American history."

"They're not mine."

"I know. This history book has Billie Jo Rendell's name in it and Jasper Dietz's is in the other. They must have left them here sometime."

Shanna frowned. "Were they close friends with Aunt Emma? I guess that they must have been to leave their books in the house."

The nurse gave a knowing laugh. "More like the two of them were taking advantage of the house being empty before you got here. They could have made good use of the place without anyone knowing."

"But how would they get in?"

"Jasper hangs out with Lew Walker a lot. The kid could have gotten the key from him. Or maybe your aunt had some extra ones. I suppose they could have lifted a key at some time when they were in the house for one reason or another. I don't know enough about your aunt to say whether or not she befriended the two of them."

The idea that her home had been used as community property didn't sit well with Shanna. She added changing all the locks to her list of priorities.

"Nice setup for kids looking for a place to make out," Marla said matter-of-factly. "They must have forgotten their school books in the heat of the moment and left them upstairs."

Was that the reason the two of them had paid her such a hurried visit? Were they worried that she'd found the books and told Billie Jo's mother about them? "Billie Jo and the boy came by, but I guess they were too scared to ask about the books. They must have lost their nerve to find out if I'd given them to her mother.''

"Well, I'll see to it that they get the books back if you want me to. I kinda of hate to see the two of them getting into more trouble. Jan and Ted aren't happy about Billie Jo taking up with someone who couldn't make it in regular high school and is going to a manual training school. Kinda slow in the brain department, but I guess he's pretty good with his hands.''

"Yes, please return the books, Marla.'' Shanna didn't want the belligerent teenagers to come around a second time.

Marla spent the next few minutes getting Holly's things settled in the sitting room. When Jay came in, he told Shanna that he'd put a lock on the basement door. "No use taking a chance that you might open it by mistake. If you need to check out anything down there, call Lew and let him do it.''

Shanna nodded. He needn't worry. A hasty look around the huge, dark cellar when she had arrived had been enough.

"Well, I think I'll be on my way," Marla said. "If there's nothing more, Dr. Jay, I'll see you at the clinic tomorrow.''

"Fine. I'll walk you to the door.''

"Thanks again, Marla.'' Shanna said.

"Glad to do it.''

Shanna could hear a whispered conversation between them as they went down the hall. She didn't need any ESP to know they were talking about her. She bit her lip. An unreasonable anger and embarrassment threatened to explode inside her. She hated being talked about like that. *Take it easy,* she scolded herself. Jay and Marla were only trying to help. They didn't mean to make her feel so inadequate. It wasn't their fault that she felt her life was completely and totally out of her control. She took a couple of deep breaths to settle her warring emotions.

Holly tested Shanna's resolution to remain calm and unruffled a moment later when she started whining for a stuffed rabbit that hadn't been unpacked since the move. "I want Bunny."

"I don't know where Bunny is, sweetheart. And Mama can't look for it right now. You have your teddy bear and your blanket—"

"I want Bunny," Holly wailed. "I want Bunny."

"You can't have Bunny," Shanna answered sharply. "Not tonight."

Holly started crying at the top of her lungs. Jay hurried back into the sitting room. "Whoa! Take it easy, kiddo. What's the matter?"

Between Holly's choked answers and Shanna's exasperated explanation, he learned that the uproar was over a missing stuffed rabbit.

"I have no idea where it is," Shanna said wearily. "In one of the unpacked boxes. But who knows which one. She has her blanket and her teddy bear—"

Holly's large woeful eyes swam with tears. "I want Bunny," she whimpered.

Jay held out his hand. "Why don't we go upstairs, Holly, and see if we can find Bunny?" The little girl sniffed, hesitated, and then put her hand in his. "Good girl. We'll be back in a few minutes," he told Shanna. "I bet we'll find that rabbit."

"Good hunting," she said in a relieved tone. Once more she was deeply grateful to this generous, caring man who was the only light in her shadowy, oppressive world.

Jiggs bounded up the steps beside Holly and Jay, and an unseen Ariel floated behind them. Shanna had made little progress in unpacking all the child's belongings during the week they'd been in the house before the accident. Nothing had been put in its proper place. Clothes, toys, bedding were piled high, and boxes of every shape and size were stacked up, waiting to be unpacked. The room was a total disaster.

After a few minutes of fruitless searching in piles and opening a dozen boxes, Holly was close to tears, and Jay was about to give up.

Ariel decided to take the matter in hand. The situation demanded some sleight-of-hand enlightenment. Angels weren't supposed to use their powers lightly, and there might be some question in heavenly quarters about the importance of a stuffed toy, but the bunny was important to Holly and that was enough for Ariel.

"What's the matter, Jiggs?" Jay asked as the dog barked excitedly and wrestled to get the lid off a shoe box that had been buried under a mound of bedding at the back of the walk-in closet. "What are you after? Get out of the way. Let me see."

Jiggs danced around in a circle, his ears flapping and his tail wagging as Jay pulled out the box and opened it.

"Well, what do you know." He laughed and patted the dog on the head. "Now, you're one smart dog. Here's the missing bunny rabbit."

Jiggs ignored Jay and poked his nose around the inside of the box, sniffing and drooling. Ariel felt a little guilty as the dog searched for the nonexistent juicy bone whose tantalizing smell had led him to the box in the far corner of the closet.

Holly's blue eyes sparkled and her pink cheeks dimpled with a broad smile as she clutched the much-loved Bunny to her chest. "Let's show Mommy."

Jay chuckled as she bobbed excitedly at his side. Her little hand felt strangely wonderful in his as they walked together down the stairs. *She's going to be as pretty as her mother,* he thought.

Ariel delighted in the loving aura suddenly radiating between the man and child. Holly didn't take to people easily, but how wonderful if this one could be a part of her life and give her the love and attention she'd never gotten from her real father. There was only one problem. Neither Jay nor Shanna were ready to commit to another marriage. Playing matchmaker between those two wasn't going to be easy. Even though they were obviously attracted to each other, Ariel knew that human emotions weren't simple.

Standing in the middle of the sitting room, Shanna could see only indistinct moving figures as they came back into the sitting room. "Any luck?"

"Jiggs found Bunny," Holly announced happily. "He knew exactly where it was."

"That's right," Jay agreed. "He led us straight to the right box. Didn't you, fellow? Just like a bloodhound following a scent."

"You have to be kidding," Shanna said, wishing she could see the twinkle that must be in Jay's eyes. So much of communication was visual, she realized. Expressions, body language, gestures and the like all added valuable insights to the spoken word.

Holly bounced up on her sofa bed. "Teddy and Bunny. Now we're a family again."

Her daughter's innocent words caused Shanna to blink back a sudden fullness in her eyes. She hoped that Jay wasn't looking at her, but when she felt his hand gently touch her arm she knew he had been watching her. "You can tell that Holly is really attached to her...family," she managed to say in a rather shaky voice.

"When I was a kid I used to carry around a stuffed frog and make croaking sounds till everyone wanted to strangle me." Jay gave a soft laugh. "I'd forgotten about my obsession until the Muppets came along with Kermit the Frog, and I felt vindicated."

"I bet you were a happy little boy."

"As happy as most, I guess. We lived in Chicago most of my growing-up days. My dad had a practice there. I guess that's why I like big cities. Lots of people. A crazy, hectic, mad rush every day."

"Any brothers or sisters?"

"No, I'm an only child."

"Me, too," she said.

"We'll have to compare notes sometime."

"Yes . . . sometime."

How little she knew about this man who had saved her life, Shanna thought. Behind the gray curtain of muted light and darkness, he was only an indistinct silhouette. What did he look like when he smiled and frowned? Was his expression as firm, as gentle, as caring, as his voice? She wanted to trace his features with her hands and make an imprint of his face in her mind's eye, but she remembered how he had withdrawn the last time she'd touched his face.

"Why are you frowning?" he asked.

"I didn't realize that I was." She wanted to know him better, much better, but she knew that her feelings about him were tainted. Her nearly blind state had created a desperate need for someone to care about her, to lessen the panic and terror of a world that was no longer familiar, and to share the traumatic experience with her. Jay Harrison filled all those needs, but she feared that her judgment of him might be as cloudy as her vision. How easy it would be to make a fool out of herself by clinging to him emotionally and physically.

"I think it's time to call it a day." She kept her body stiff and unyielding even as his nearness invited her to lean into him.

"Yes, I should be going...unless you want me to stay and tuck both of you in?"

"No, I'm in good shape now to handle things," she assured him. "Thanks to you and Marla, there shouldn't be any real problems."

"Why don't I come by for breakfast in the morning?" he suggested lightly. "I can make coffee and open a box of cereal with the best of them."

"No," she said with blunt firmness. "I appreciate the offer, but you've done quite enough already. More than enough, really. You have certainly demonstrated your professional commitment. Looking after me in the hospital, making house calls."

"Professional commitment? House calls?"

She didn't have to see his face to know that her words had angered him. She apologized quickly, "I'm sorry, I just—"

"Sounds to me like you're expecting me to bill you for services rendered," he flared.

"Of course not, it's just that you're a doctor and...and you've been more than generous with your time."

"If you think I'm going to waltz out of your life and let you go this alone, you're way off base. You can't dismiss me because I'm not your doctor." A faint smile curved her lips and her mouth was so damn kissable that he added gruffly, "And I want you to promise me that you won't be so damn proud that you won't accept my help when you need it."

As she lifted her chin, he mentally traced its firm and stubborn line with his eyes. He knew that her skin would be warm and soft beneath his touch. His fingers itched to thread themselves in the lovely golden-red curls falling around her face and lying gently on her shoulders. A soft white T-shirt molded her breasts with a tantalizing invitation for him to reach out and touch their nippled peaks. His voice was gruff as he said, "I have to go back to Denver tomorrow, but I'll see you before I leave. If you need me before that, call me tonight at my dad's place, or at the clinic tomorrow. Promise?"

"I promise, but I'll be just fine."

Her confident assurance was at odds with a slight wavering in her voice. Shadows marred her delicately boned cheeks, and weary lines etched her mouth. Her posture was rigid and unyielding, and yet the valiant woman standing before him cried out to be caressed and loved.

Dammit, he swore silently as a surge of sexual desire coursed through him. Her half-parted lips begged to be kissed. The rise and fall of her breasts taunted him. His hands ached to mold the curves of her waist and hips. Until that moment, he had never desired a woman with such compelling hunger. He wanted to take her to bed and hold her tenderly and passionately till morning.

The whole situation was impossible. He had to put distance between himself and Shanna Ryan before he let himself get emotionally involved. She'd already made it quite plain that she didn't want him intruding in her life, and he certainly wasn't going to allow her to break down all the protective barriers he'd carefully put in place after his divorce.

"Good night, then," he said gruffly.

"'Night," Holly said unexpectedly from her bed.

With a pleased chuckle, Jay walked over to the sofa bed and gave the child a light kiss on the cheek. Then he said, "Good night, Mr. Teddy. Good night, Mr. Bunny. Sleep tight."

His tenderness toward Holly brought down every shred of pride Shanna had raised against him. Her breath lodged like a lump in her throat. If he had turned and taken her in his arms at that moment, she would have willingly gone to him.

The moment passed. She felt like someone suddenly dipped in chipped ice when he walked by her. "Good night, Shanna," he said from the hall doorway.

Her lower lips trembled. "Good night." A moment later she heard the front door close and his car drive off.

She was on her own, just the way she'd always been.

ARIEL SLIPPED INTO the car with Jay as he drove to Deerview, the property his father had bought along Miners Creek about five miles west of town. His dad was proud of the Deerview acreage, which included a modest log house, barn and horse pasture. The large meadow was a favorite grazing spot for mule-eared deer and had given the property its name. Prospectors had panned for gold in the nearby creek, and high on the moutainside, tailings remained where hopeful miners had brought out ore in wheelbarrows and buckets. His dad loved to talk about the Old West as if he, too, had shared in it.

By the time Jay pulled up in front of the small log house, twilight had already settled in the narrow mountain valley, tinting thick stands of conifer and aspen trees in shades of mauve and purple. A sleek black horse lifted his head in a nearby pasture as Jay got out of the car and walked over to the fence. Ariel's weakness for horses brought a silent cry of delight as the animal clomped over to them. As Jay rubbed the horse's neck and talked to it, Ariel perched on his back and ruffled his mane and tail with wisps of soft wind.

"How you doing, Johnny? Is old man Jacobs looking after you all right? Bet you miss Pops. He keeps asking if I've taken you out for a gallop." Jay laughed to himself, admitting that he'd rather leap on a subway train roaring out of the station than climb up on this fellow's back. "Guess you'll have to wait a little while longer, Johnny, for a good run." He gave the horse a final pat.

As Jay walked toward the house, he could hear swiftly flowing waters of the nearby creek and for a brief moment regretted that he didn't have his father's love of fishing. Even though he'd tried fly-fishing a few times, his efforts had been a waste of time. Fishing and riding horses were definitely not at the top of his list of things to do.

"You need a hobby," his father had told him more than once, but he didn't have time for a hobby. Night and day, his beeper was a constant taskmaster, bringing him back to the hospital even when he was supposed to have a few hours off. And that's the way he liked it, especially now that he rattled around in the ultramodern flat Valerie had insisted on buying. He hated the way she'd decorated it. Stark white with red-and-black accents. Someday he'd get around to redecorating the place—if he didn't sell it first.

His dad's log house was small and compact and would have fit into half of his New York apartment. The front door opened into one long room with a fireplace at one end. There was a small kitchen and two bedrooms with a connecting bath. Jay tossed his stuff in the back room where he'd been staying on his weekly trips to Westridge.

Perching unseen on a kitchen counter, Ariel watched him search the cupboard for something to eat and finally decide on a can of Dinty Moore stew for dinner. He heated it, and then took his bowl and a can of beer into the living room. He put a couple of logs in the fireplace and coaxed them into a warm, bright flame. Then he sat on the sofa, eating his stew and staring at the fire.

Ariel settled down on the raised brick hearth and studied his face. She knew that often mortals wore a mask when they were with other people, but when they were alone, they dropped their pretense and it was easier to see into their hearts. Watching him with Shanna and Holly told her a few things about him, but she didn't know how committed he might be to staying in Colorado. He could up and leave at any moment, and where would that leave her? *Without the human partner she needed.* Somehow she had to convince him that it was imperative for him to stay close to Shanna. Now was a good time to see if he was receptive to thought transference.

She willed her voice inside his head. *Call your father and tell him you're not going home tomorrow.*

She waited. Nothing happened.

She tried a second time. Again nothing happened. Maybe she was doing something wrong. She knew that thoughts were energy impulses. Maybe Jay's subconscious wasn't going to allow the fine filament of dendrites in his brain cells to pick up these transmitted impulses. He could effectively shut them out of his consciousness, and there was nothing she could do about it. Few earthlings made use of the sixth sense that would allow them to transmit and receive telepathic messages.

Jay got up, went to the kitchen, put his dirty bowl in the sink and then took another can of beer out of the refrigerator. He was as oblivious as a blind and deaf man in the presence of a full orchestra.

Maybe she should look for someone else. If Jay was determined to block out any psychic awareness and refused to act on any intuitive impulses, he would be of little use to her. If the wires were down, they were down.

She watched him as he sat staring into the fire and drinking his beer. He was worried about Shanna, she could tell that. All he needed was a little shove in the right direction. Ariel was certain that once he became aware of the vicious attempt on Shanna's life, he would be more than ready to protect her and Holly.

She increased the level of her psychic transmission and tried again. *You have to stay in Westridge. Call your father and tell him so.*

Jay got up and walked right by the phone and into the kitchen. He washed up his few dishes and then went outside. As he leaned up against the porch railing he stared up at an eyelash of a moon.

Ariel didn't know what to do next. How could she and Jay work together as a sleuthing team if he blocked her out of his mind? She was trying to decide what to do next when suddenly Jay pushed to his feet, went back inside and went straight to the telephone.

Ariel shouted "hallelujah" as he dialed his father's number.

"Dad, I think I'll spend an extra night in Westridge if you're doing all right."

"Sure, son. Going fishing, are you?"

Jay laughed. He knew his father had always squeezed in a little fishing on his weekly trips to Westridge. "No, I'm waiting for you to show me the best spots. Marla said you'd better hurry up because the fishing's good now in the creek."

"Well, it won't be long now. I'm getting my legs back under me. How's Johnny? Is old man Winters taking good care of him?"

"He looks fine."

"Probably getting fat from no exercise. He needs to be taken on a good run. Don't suppose you'd want to saddle him up? Take him for a few turns around the pasture just to loosen him up?"

"Now, Dad, I barely know which side to mount, and I'm respectful of Johnny's horse sense. Not for one minute would I fool him into thinking I could stay in the saddle if he decided to dump me."

His father sighed. "I suppose not. How are things at the clinic?"

"Busy. Everyone asks about you."

"Any emergencies?"

"No. Everything's under control." Jay knew his father was waiting for some further explanation for his decision to stay. From the beginning, Jay had been honest about his lack of enthusiasm for the small mountain community. This sudden decision to spend an extra night must be puzzling his dad. In fact, it puzzled Jay, too.

"How's the Ryan woman?" his father asked with infuriating perception.

"Her name is Shanna, and she's getting settled in. Marla and I spent a lot of time trying to make things easier for her." He told his dad how they had rearranged furniture and put braille dots on knobs and switches. "She's going to live in the downstairs rooms until her vision improves. I'm sure she'll be able to handle things."

"But?" his father prodded.

Jay chuckled. "All right, Dad. I admit it. I'm worried about her. That rambling house would be a challenge for someone with full sight. And she's so damn stubborn that she won't admit how vulnerable she is. There are a hundred ways she could hurt herself. I just feel better being close by."

"Sounds to me like you're getting emotionally involved, son," Bradley warned. "Better step back a little."

"I can't. Not until Shanna's capable of looking out for herself again."

"Sounds serious. What are you planning to do? Move in with her until she gets her sight back?"

"She'd never agree to anything like that. I just think I ought to stay close, at least for a couple of days."

"A couple of days isn't going to see much improvement in her physical condition, is it?"

"No. The specialist isn't saying how long it will take for a full recovery."

"Sounds to me like you're setting yourself up for a very unprofessional relationship with this gal. I'd be careful if I were you, son. She's undoubtedly feeling insecure, and it'd be damn easy for her to play on your emotions."

"Shanna wouldn't do that. She's not the least bit manipulative. In fact, I've never met anyone who was so determined to be completely independent. And that's what worries me. I have the feeling that she won't ask for help from me or Marla unless we keep tabs on her."

His father grunted. "Well, do what you think best, but remember, saving the woman's life doesn't obligate you to anything. And if she's as strong as you say, she's going to take your concern as interference. You may be setting yourself up for an unpleasant situation."

"I'll have to take that chance."

They talked for a few more minutes about his father's health, and Jay was reassured that he was in good hands with a live-in male nurse that Jay had hired. For the first time, his dad actually mentioned retiring.

"I think Dr. Morrison would be willing to take over my practice permanently. Of course, you know I'd be happy if you decided to stick around—"

"Thanks, Dad, but we've been all over that."

"Well, if you're sure you want to go back to that big city rat race," he hedged. "But the Colorado Rockies are a good place for a man to meet his inner self. Maybe, get his priorities straight.''

Ariel listened to the conversation with a smile. Maybe she had an ally in the older doctor.

After Jay hung up the phone, he sat down in front of the fireplace and stared at the flickering flames. Ariel sensed his loneliness and settled unseen on the couch beside him, snuggling close the way Holly would have done.

He sighed, leaned his head back on the couch and closed his eyes. She wished he could know that she was there beside him. Mortal children didn't realize how lucky they were. They didn't always appreciate being hugged and kissed and tickled. Holly would have been able to crawl up on his lap and cuddle in his arms. The best that Ariel could do was surround him in an aura of warm tenderness as she let her angelic heart expand with thoughts of what might happen if Jay and Shanna and Holly became a family.

As if her psychic musing got through to him, Jay got up. He picked up the phone and then set it back down again. ''She's probably in bed by now,'' he muttered.

Call her, anyway.

But he didn't.

Once more, Ariel entertained a flicker of apprehension. Jay's strong-willed psyche could mean trouble. She wished he was as pliable as Holly... and Jiggs.

Jay took a book off the shelf and plopped down on the sofa again. Only he didn't seem to be able to concentrate, Ariel noticed. He'd stare at a page for ten times as long as it would take to read it.

''Blast it all,'' he swore, and slammed the book shut. He got up, poked at the fire, and restlessly wandered around the room. Time hanging heavy on his hands was a new experience for him. Usually he needed to be in at least two places at once.

When he spied his father's guitar leaning up against the wall in a corner of the room, he gave in to an impulse and picked it up. He smiled, remembering how his father had taught him a few simple songs when he was in high school. Did he remember any of them? He brought the old guitar back to the sofa and began to strum a few chords.

Ariel was delighted. She loved music, any kind, even Holly's cute little ditties, "Pop Goes The Weasel" and "London Bridge." She always sang along with Holly's little record player, and the two of them would whirl around the room in an abandoned dance until they both collapsed with laughter.

She swept over to the sofa beside him as Jay strummed some remembered chords. After much fumbling, he chuckled aloud when he found the right notes for "Red River Valley" and began to sing in his rich baritone voice. "Come sit by my side if you love me."

Ariel laughed and raised her pure voice in harmony with his. "Do not hasten to bid me adieu."

Jay was amazed how well and easily the remembered songs came to him. It had been years since he'd had a guitar in his hands. He couldn't even remember what had happened to the one his parents had given him for Christmas one year. He'd been too busy pursuing his career to even think about fooling around with a guitar. As he played and sang, and the small room vibrated with duets that only Ariel could hear, he bowed to an unseen audience and offered an enthusiastic rendition of "The Yellow Rose of Texas."

He couldn't believe how nimble his fingers were, how deftly he strummed the chords that seemed to flow so easily from his memory. After nearly an hour of singing and playing, he laughingly put the guitar back in its corner. It had been years since he'd had time for such idle enjoyment. He'd been caught up in his work, and Valerie had been caught up in her social whirl. Neither of them had had time for a family, and in the end, they hadn't had time for each other.

He thought about Shanna and the refreshing evening he'd spent in the isolated mountain valley. For the first time in his life he wondered if he'd been running too fast to let happiness catch up with him.

JOHNNY WAS STILL HANGING his head over the fence rail as if waiting for someone to give him some attention when Ariel left the house. She obliged the horse by perching on the fence and stroking him.

"You miss your master, don't you, fellow."

Johnny flung his head upward, and neighed pitifully.

She stroked his neck, and he looked at her with large brown eyes that begged, *Let's go for a ride.*

I really shouldn't, she told herself, but only half-heartedly. One of her secret longings had always been to ride a winged steed across the sky like a shooting star, but even a horseback ride around an earthly pasture would be great fun.

He neighed again and she laughed. "All right." A split second later she was sitting astride his back.

Like a flash of moonlight, horse and rider streaked across the pasture, sailed smoothly over the fence and bounded up a mountain trail to a high precipice that rose to touch the heavens.

Chapter Five

Ariel had just put Johnny back in the pasture when she picked up Shanna's telepathic panic. Like the bright light of a comet, she flew back to the house.

A few minutes earlier Shanna had been lying stiffly in bed staring at the ceiling. A patch of an indistinct night-light came through the open door from the sitting room where Holly was sleeping. The events of the day swirled through her mind like dry leaves whipping in the wind, and the night sounds in the house seemed to be alive and breathing. Even though she knew the upstairs rooms were empty, shifting floorboards, the rattling of window frames and echoing whispers grated on her nerves.

Jiggs suddenly gave a low growl and lifted his head from the rug on which he was lying beside her bed. Then he bounded out of the room.

Shanna stiffened. Jiggs had never been much of a watchdog. A stray cat or barking neighborhood dog were about the only incentives for him to go storming around the house like a ferocious beast. Most of the time he wagged his tail and woofed happily at anyone who walked into the house. She could hear him now scratching at the front door.

She swung her legs over the side of the bed. Her mouth was suddenly dry and her pulse rapid.

"Jiggs, come here!" It was past one o'clock in the morning. Who would be at the front door at this hour? Jay? Had he realized that she was lying awake, thinking about him?

With outstretched hands, she moved forward until she touched a chest of drawers that Jay had placed on the left side of the hall door. She felt her way along the top of the chest and then reached out and touched the doorframe.

Don't panic. Take it slow.

With her hands feeling the air in front of her, she moved out into the hall. Then she turned and walked toward the front of the house, letting one hand run along the wall the way Jay had instructed.

Jiggs stopped his barking and came running back to her, bounding about her legs as if pleased with himself.

"Yes, who is it?" she called out as she reached the front door. Silence. Her hope that it might be Jay coming to check on her faded. She bent her head close to the glass in the front door and listened. A creaking that might have been the wind moving Aunt Emma's porch rocker was her only answer. Had something or somebody been on the porch? Or in the house?

She checked the door and discovered it was unlocked. "I know I locked it. How did it get unlocked?"

Someone with a key.

Sweat beaded on her forehead.

Had someone let themselves in?

Billie Jo and Jasper? Had they come back for their books, not knowing that Marla would be returning them to them?

"Was someone coming in the house when you heard them?" she asked Jiggs as if the tail-wagging mutt could answer. Her mouth went dry. "Or was someone in the house before you heard them?"

A flash of stabbing light accompanied Ariel's return to the house and for a brief second the front hall was illuminated like a flash of summer lightning. The brilliance came and went so fast that Shanna wasn't sure she'd seen it.

In an instant, Ariel made a flying tour of the house, from attic to cellar. She picked up a lingering dark aura in the kitchen and on the front stairs. And whoever it was had spent enough time in the house to leave behind a psychic impression. The same lingering vibrations were on the front porch. Jiggs must have heard the intruder as he was leaving.

Nothing seemed out of place, and yet the miasma of evil remained. Someone had been in the house.

Doing what?

SHANNA SPENT A RESTLESS night, and she had just finished dressing the next morning and started down the hall toward the kitchen when the doorbell rang. As she turned around Jiggs came racing out of Holly's room, nearly knocking Shanna over in his scramble toward the front door.

Who could that be? The uneasiness of last night's unlocked door remained, even though she had almost convinced herself that she hadn't properly turned the lock when she went to bed. Heaven knows, there was nothing in the house worth anybody's time stealing.

And if one of the teenagers had come back for the books, they had probably been shaking in their shoes the whole time.

"Shut up, Jiggs," Shanna commanded. She didn't want the dog to wake up Holly, who was always fussy when she didn't get all her sleep. The way the dog was bouncing around her legs as she felt her way along the wall, she'd be lucky if she didn't fall flat on her face.

Jay shifted his weight on the front porch and peered through the door glass. He was relieved when he saw Shanna moving cautiously across the front hall with her hands extended out in front of her. Good, she was up and about. He had been worried that she might have been so completely overwhelmed after yesterday's traumatic experiences that she wouldn't even want to get out of bed. He should have known better.

"It's me, Jay," he called. As she turned the lock and slowly opened the door, he stuck his head in. "Good morning. It's room service. Coffee and Danish delivered to your doorstep."

A relieved smile brightened her face, "Come in." She was glad he hadn't taken her at her word when she told him not to come for breakfast. "I was just heading for the kitchen to launch an assault on the coffee maker."

"Then I'm glad I got here just in time. The Busy Bee Café was happy to fill my thermos and send along some freshly baked Danish. He deliberately passed the sack in front of her nose. "Take a whiff of those tempting smells."

"Hmm." She sighed. "Heaven!"

Jiggs danced around Jay's legs with welcoming joy as if the sack in his hand held something for him. He gave the dog's head a pat and then took Shanna's arm. "May I escort you, milady?"

As they walked toward the kitchen, Jay searched her face. Not a good night, he thought. Her mouth was tense and weary, and those lines still marred her forehead. As she walked beside him, her movement was uneasy, unsure. Dammit, she'd told him to stay away and he'd almost taken her at her word. He wasn't used to forcing his presence on anyone, especially a woman as blasted proud and stubborn as Shanna Ryan. She'd been pretty emphatic about not wanting him to come and fix breakfast. A half-dozen times he'd changed his mind about dropping by, but in the end the need to reassure himself that she was all right overrode his hesitation. "I didn't come too early, did I?"

She shook her head. "I've been awake since my clock announced five o'clock. I lay there with my eyes closed, half believing when I opened them, I would be able to see everything clearly again."

"That'll happen," he assured her as he guided her to a kitchen chair. "Not all at once, though. And we don't know how soon."

She felt a rise of unreasonable irritation. Didn't he realize that even one minute trapped in shadowy blindness was an eternity to her? "It can't be soon enough."

"You'll just have to be patient."

She gave a self-mocking laugh. "Patience has never been a virtue of mine. I hate standing in lines, waiting for traffic lights to change, and people who are always late really bug me. I've always preferred to do things myself than wait for someone else to do them."

"A typical Type A personality," he chided, and then chuckled as he confessed, "Patience isn't my long suit, either. Maybe at heart, we're two of a kind. What do you think?''

"Isn't this where we compare horoscopes?" she teased. "Really, Doctor, I would have expected more from you. You must have a better line than that?"

"Well, I'm out of practice. Now, what kind of Danish would you like? We have three choices of fruit topping—strawberry, peach or apple."

"Holly likes strawberry," Shanna said, automatically looking out for her daughter. "And I like all of them."

He placed the apple Danish in front of her. "And I bet you like your coffee black."

"Wrong. I take both sugar and cream."

"Not a purist, I gather?"

"Not about food."

"About other things?"

She paused. "Yes, I guess you could say that. I like my relationships with other people to be genuine." He watched her hands tighten around her coffee mug. "I don't like playing pretend games...especially with those I care about. I want to know where I stand."

Her words were a challenge thrown smack in his face. His ambivalence, his wavering between a professional concern and a personal caring had come through to her loud and clear. She was too damn perceptive. She wanted an honesty from him that he couldn't even give to himself, let alone her.

He sat down across the table from her. All his life he'd had a protective shield between himself and those closest to him, but he was weary of being alone and gave in to the strange impulse to share his private self with her.

"I can't remember who first decided that I should become a doctor. My mother, probably. She was a totally sweet, wonderful person who never raised her voice but somehow managed everyone with iron persuasion. I can't remember my dad pushing me into medicine, but all through school Mom praised me for bringing home good grades and setting good goals. By the time she passed away from breast cancer the year I graduated from university, I had already been accepted to medical school. To make her proud of me I strove to be the most dedicated, successful and prosperous physician in New York City."

In the heavy silence that followed, she asked, "And you achieved your goals?"

"Oh, yes, indeed. I've given everything to my work, and it's paid off royally. My achievements, my reputation and my bank account speak well for my career." Then he gave a mocking laugh. "But I definitely have flunked almost every other area of my life. I guess I've been guilty of playing a role when it came to anything outside my work. I know now that there's no room in my life for personal relationships." He reached over and took her hand. "As much as I'd like to forget about who I am and give my feelings free rein, I can't."

"Please don't think I was inviting any continuing interest in me," Shanna said stiffly. "I didn't mean to suggest that there was anything false about you. You've been a true and valuable friend, Dr. Harrison."

Dr. Harrison! The formal use of his name mocked him. "I thought we were on a first-name basis," he chided. "You know, like friends."

"Friends? I don't have much to offer in a friend-ship at the moment."

"You have a great deal to offer," he countered bluntly. "I certainly didn't mean to suggest that I'm not open to enjoying your companionship while I'm in Westridge. I just meant that in a short time I'll be back at Manhattan General, caught up in the chaotic life of my choosing."

"I know. And as soon as my vision returns I'll be caught up in my own goals. You see, I've never had a chance to develop my own talents. My husband didn't want me to be the least bit independent. I came to the marriage with no skills and he liked it that way. He seemed to be attracted to other career women, but he didn't want one for a wife."

She's been deeply hurt, he thought, watching as a flicker of deep pain crossed her face. Jay felt himself getting angry at a man he'd never met.

During the exchange between the two adults, Ariel lounged beside Jiggs on his rug in the corner and scratched his floppy ears as he sprawled contentedly beside her. As she listened intently to the conversa-tional exchanges between the doctor and Shanna, she was disappointed. They were covering up thoughts and feelings that had little relationship to the words com-ing out of their mouths.

Shanna obviously liked Jay Harrison. She always had a soft smile on her lips when she looked in his di-rection and narrowed her eyes as if hoping to bring him into better focus. And the doctor was clearly taken with her, thought Ariel, completely mystified as to why the two of them were erecting invisible walls against each other. Human behavior was certainly baffling at times. I have my work cut out for me, thought Ariel, if I want to play Cupid to these two.

"Well, I'd better be getting to the clinic," Jay said as he pushed back his chair. "Marla will have my neck if I don't get the paperwork done before it opens. We are usually busier on the second day I'm here. I'll be heading back to Denver about four o'clock."

Shanna found her mouth suddenly dry. "And you'll be back next Monday and Tuesday?"

"That's the usual schedule." He waited for her to say something that would persuade him to stick around and make a pest of himself. When she didn't, he paused beside her chair. "I guess you'll be all right till I come back next week."

Why doesn't she tell him about last night? Ariel sent out a strong telepathic suggestion, but Shanna was not receiving. "I'll be fine," she said, standing up and facing him.

She looked so bravely vulnerable that he wanted to take her in his arms. He didn't know how it had happened, but this brave and devastatingly appealing woman had opened up facets of tenderness and needs deep within himself he'd never felt before. He didn't want to leave her, not for an hour, not for a day, certainly not for a week. But such feelings were idiotic and completely irrational. He felt as though he'd been pulled in so many different warring directions at once.

The lines in her forehead deepened as she struggled to bring him into focus. "Thanks for coming by."

"My pleasure." He quickly touched her shoulder and then pulled away before his hand could linger on her soft warmth. "Listen, we have an ophthalmoscope at the clinic. I know you're not scheduled for a Denver checkup for ten days, but it wouldn't hurt to have a look at those eyes. There may be signs that the liquid is already being absorbed.''

''That would be good news,'' she admitted.

''Marla should be free enough some time during the day to come up and get you.''

''No need. Holly and I can walk down to Main Street.''

''You'll need to be very careful. It's imperative that you don't injure yourself again.''

''Don't worry. I'm not going to do anything reckless, but there are certain things I must do. I can't make a hothouse flower out of Holly. That means I have to develop some confidence about moving around outside as well as in.''

He sighed. There was that stubborn streak again. ''All right, do it your way. I'll plan on seeing you later today.'' He got up from the table.

''Wait a minute, I'll walk you to the door.''

''Show off!'' he teased.

She boldly slipped her arm through his, loving the feel of his masculine body brushing against hers. As they lingered at the front door, Ariel decided it was time to do something to make Shanna confide in Jay about last night's intruder.

But what?

Shanna was not like Holly, who had little trouble accepting the existence of things-not-seen and relating to forces-not-understood. Shanna was cautious about the things she did and said. Hiding her insecurity had become a way of life for her. No telling how long it would be before she let Jay know what had happened the night before.

But he needs to know. Ariel focused on sending a message deep inside Jay's awareness. *She's hiding something from you.*

A frown crossed his face.

Ask her what she'd holding back.

"Shanna?"

"Yes?"

"What is it? What aren't you telling me?"

"I don't know what you mean."

"There's something, I feel it," Jay insisted. "Tell me, Shanna. You're holding something back, aren't you?"

Shanna hesitated for a long moment before she nodded. "Last night, Jiggs heard something. And I found the front door unlocked."

Jay wanted to lash out at her for not telling him sooner, but he managed to ask evenly, "What time was this?"

"Sometime after midnight. About one o'clock, I think. I don't know if I'd just dropped off to sleep or not. Anyway, Jiggs ran to the front door, jumping and scratching the way he does when he wants out."

"And did you let him out?"

"No. By the time I got to the door, he'd quieted down. The funny thing is, the door was unlocked."

"Didn't you lock up before you went to bed?"

"I thought I had it locked. The door doesn't have a bolt. Just a key. Anyway, I don't really think anyone came in...."

Wrong, Ariel silently corrected. *The intruder's lingering aura was all over the house.*

The demanding ring of the telephone cut short the rest of her sentence. Jay picked up the phone off the nearby hall table and handed it to her.

"Hello?" Shanna answered in a puzzled voice. Who would be calling her?

"Listen carefully, Shanna Ryan," said a deep, muffled voice. "Leave Westridge. Or your next accident will kill you."

Shanna raised a hand to her mouth, stifling a gasp.

"What is it?" Jay grabbed the phone from her in time to hear the click of a receiver. "What the—?"

Shanna's face had bleached to a pasty white. Her slender body quivered as if she had suddenly fallen ill with a deadly chill.

"Who was it? Tell me. What did he say?"

Her lips move in a quavering whisper as she repeated the vicious warning. She closed her eyes in horror. "Why would someone give me a message like that?"

"I...I'm not sure," Jay hedged. *Next accident!* The threat vibrated in his head with the deafening clash of cymbals, but to Ariel's disappointment, he shoved the suspicion away. No, it was too farfetched. Some nut could just be using the situation to his advantage. The newspapers are full of stories about people who take credit for happenings so they can benefit in some way.

"The authorities need to know about this. I'm betting there's some nut living around here who has a record of making sadistic calls like this."

He pulled her to him and held her tightly as a shiver rippled down her back. "It's going to be all right," he promised. "We'll put a stop to this harassment in short order. Maybe you should stay inside until—"

"No," she said, pulling away. "Some lunatic isn't going to make me a prisoner in my own house."

He opened his mouth to argue, and then closed it. She was right. Any sign of weakness only encouraged creeps who got their kicks out of instilling fear in their victims.

The hardest thing he ever had to do was turn away and leave her standing in the doorway. He went directly to the deputy's one-man office in a small brick building housing a two-cell jail.

Ariel, who'd followed him, was excited about her first visit to an honest-to-goodness jail, but after a cursory look around, the small office and even tinier cells were disappointing, especially after the big prisons she'd seen on late-night television.

The lawman was a disappointment, too. He'd didn't look a bit like Clint Eastwood. He was sandy-haired, short, pudgy, with a mustache of powdered sugar around a big fleshy mouth.

Jay had never met Deputy Skaggs before. From what he'd heard, the old law officer didn't cut a very authoritative figure in the town, but the sheriff's office was in Cedarville, the county seat, about fifty miles away. Marla had said Deputy Skaggs was rather lazy but good enough to handle Saturday night drunks and the fistfights that erupted in the back rooms of the Timberline Bar. Skaggs had never been in the clinic since Jay had been filling in for his father.

Jay's first impression of the law officer was less than complimentary. The deputy, his feet up on the corner of his desk, was eating a powdered doughnut and reading a Denver newspaper when Jay came into the office.

"Deputy Skaggs?" Jay asked doubtfully even though a badge on the rumpled western shirt seemed authentic enough.

Skaggs lowered the paper, and his bushy eyebrows furrowed as he grunted, "That's right."

"I'm Dr. Harrison. I need to talk to you about Shanna Ryan."

Skaggs clumsily put his feet down and shifted his fat buttocks in the squeaky desk chair. "Shanna Ryan? Miss Emma's niece? The gal who moved into her house with her kid?"

"You know about her car going off the road about ten days ago?"

"Of course I know," he snapped, tipping way back in his chair. "The highway patrol's report listed excessive speed as the cause. Hell, I could have told them that. Crazy bunch of drivers. Happens all the time. Gunning down one of them freeways ain't the same as mountain driving."

"The accelerator stuck on Mrs. Ryan's car. That's why she couldn't keep it under control, and why it went over the cliff."

Skaggs looked skeptical and then shrugged. "Same difference. Too much speed."

"Last night, someone could have been snooping around her house, and a few minutes ago she got a hate call."

"A hate call?" Skaggs repeated as if he hadn't heard the term before.

Jay repeated the message word for word, putting emphasis on the menace of "Leave Westridge. Or your next accident will kill you."

Skaggs shrugged and leaned back in his squeaky chair as if he was more interested in reading his morning paper than in Shanna's telephone call.

"Do you have some psycho in the area who makes calls like that?"

"Nope."

"Well, somebody made this one." The man's indifference was infuriating. "Isn't it your business to find out who?" The sarcasm was lost on Skaggs.

"Could be a lot of people," he mumbled, wiping at his sugary mouth. "Folks around here don't take to newcomers moving in and changing things. We got a nice quiet little community here. Until them Texans moved in we had the fish and deer all to ourselves."

"That's beside the point." Jay leaned over the desk. "Mrs. Ryan received a threatening telephone call. What are you going to do about it?"

Skaggs looked down his bulbous nose at Jay. "Word is that this Mrs. Ryan is aiming to fix that old house up into some kind of a fancy inn. Maybe somebody doesn't like the idea."

Ariel was afraid that Jay was going to reach over and throttle the man. "I want to talk with your superior," Jay said in an ice-cold, professional manner.

"What?"

"Your superior. What's the sheriff's name? I want to talk to him."

Skaggs's fleshy face colored. "*I* handle matters in Westridge. And I don't like some city dude coming in here telling me how to do my job."

"Then I'll contact the sheriff myself."

"That will do you little good, seeing he's on a month's leave." He glared at Jay. "It's me or nobody, Doctor. If you want me to look into this thing—"

"Of course I want you to look into it." *Why in the hell does he think I came here?* "Aren't you supposed to make out a report on something like this?"

"Don't be telling me how to do my job."

Somebody should, thought Jay, and Ariel agreed with him. She wished Jay would focus more on Shanna's car accident. As if he were becoming more receptive to their intuitive communication, he verbalized the thought. "Maybe we should focus on Shanna's car accident?"

"Don't see what that has to do with anything."

Ariel wanted to bop him in his thick skull. She'd seen Jiggs comprehend things faster than this guy. If the dense deputy convinced Jay that his suspicions were unfounded, she'd be back to square one again with no mortal knowing what she did—that someone had tampered with the car.

Jay rose to his feet. "Sorry to have taken up your time." He started toward the door.

No, no, don't leave.

Changing his mind, he came back, put his hands on Skaggs's desk and leaned over so he was only a few inches from the man's face. "What if the caller fixed the accelerator on Mrs. Ryan's car? What if you have a killer loose in your nice little community?" Jay demanded.

The deputy tried to move back from Jay's accusing face and nearly tipped his chair over. His face reddened again. "Don't be looking for big city violence around here, Doctor. This ain't New York. We have a nice little town here, and I aim to keep it that way."

Jay kept his steady gaze on Skaggs's flushed face. "The accelerator on Shanna's car stuck. The caller warned her that her *next* accident would kill her. What are you going to do to protect Shanna Ryan from—"

"From what?" Skaggs snapped and lurched to his feet. "From being fool enough to drive like a bat out of hell down a mountain road? Let me tell you something, mister." His red cheeks looked ready to pop. "Nobody fixed her car. The guy that made that call is just trying to warn her that she doesn't belong in a place like this. Darn good advice. No telling what damn fool thing she'll do next."

For a moment, Jay looked as if he might put his hands around Skaggs's thick neck and throttle him. Ariel was relieved when Jay took a deep breath and said, "You'd better make damn sure the sheriff gets a report on this."

"And you'd better stick to doctoring. I've lived in Westridge all my life and don't need any Texans or city slickers, telling me what to do. You got that?"

"Yes, Deputy, I got it, plain and clear." Jay turned and walked out of the office. The man was about as narrow-minded, prejudiced and dense as they came.

Ariel was disappointed that they weren't going to get any help from the law, but things could be worse. At least, now that Jay was aware of the real situation, she had a human ally in ferreting out the truth.

Ariel kept close to Jay's side as he strode across the street to the clinic. She wished he could know that she was there. They were partners, a team, working together to keep Shanna and Holly from danger. Even though he was unaware of her childish touch, she slipped her hand into his and started humming one of the songs they'd sung together the night before. She was pleased when the tension in his body eased.

Maybe he sensed he wasn't alone.

Chapter Six

At about three o'clock in the afternoon, Shanna shut Jiggs up on the back porch and, holding on to Holly's hand, started walking down the hill toward Main Street. The sun was bright and warm, but shifting patterns of dark and light in Shanna's vision still made it impossible to see anything around her clearly. Navigating a rutted dirt road bordered on both sides by thick drifts of conifer wasn't as easy as she had expected. Her feet seemed to find every uneven spot and rock along the way, and Holly kept trying to pull her along at a faster pace.

"Come on, Mama. Ariel's going to beat us to the bottom of the hill."

Shanna choked back a sharp reply. This was no time to play games with Holly's imaginary friend. Shanna was used to including the unseen playmate in the family's activities, but at the moment, make-believe games were out of the question. Under normal circumstances she probably would have humored her daughter and pretended to engage in a three-way race down the hill. "No races, today, Holly. Tell Ariel she'll have to play with someone else until Mama gets better."

"Who?"

"I don't know. Some other little girl who needs a playmate."

"But what if Ariel likes her better than me?"

Shanna drew in an exasperated breath. How on earth did she get into this ridiculous conversation? With all the weighty problems in her mind, she didn't need this kind of an argument about a playmate that didn't exist. Maybe she'd made a mistake in not putting the brakes on Holly's imagination when she first started talking about her new friend. But how could she have known that the pretense would last this long? Children were supposed to grow out of such fantasies. Now she was faced with the problem of convincing Holly that it was time to give up this figment of her imagination. Coping with reality was challenge enough.

Holly tugged on her hand. "Mama?"

"Yes?"

"Ariel says she doesn't want to go play with anybody else. She's going to stay with us."

There was such relief in Holly's voice that Shanna made herself say, "That's nice." She'd go along with the pretense at least for a little while longer until the moment was right to have a talk about make-believe and things that were real.

Main Street's sidewalk made for easier footing, but Shanna still stumbled against cracks and dips in the old, settling concrete. She wished that she had paid more attention to things the few days she'd been in town before the accident. The business district was three blocks long with lots of vacant buildings and only a few year-round establishments, including a café, a bar, a country grocery, a gas station and a small mercantile store.

The clinic was in an old brick building next to the Timberline Bar. Shanna's nose caught odors of stale beer and cigarette smoke as they passed it. She slowed down, hesitating as she heard someone come out of a door just ahead.

"Is this the Westridge Clinic?" she asked the unseen person.

"Yep. Sure is," answered a man with a western twang. A rough, callused hand grabbed hers. "Ted Rendell. My wife told me you'd been in a car accident. Sure am sorry about your eyes. Must be pretty awful being blind."

"I'm not blind. My vision is just cloudy. I don't see people's faces very clearly."

"Well, in my case, that's a blessing." He gave a hearty chuckle. "Folks say my mug's homelier than a hog routing in the mud. Beats all how I happened to lasso a filly like Janet. You're mighty pretty yourself, if you don't mind me saying so."

Was he just being a friendly old boy or was he coming on to her? Shanna was wary of her new neighbors. Janet was pushy and calculating, but her husband might be a different sort. She wished she could see him. He sounded tall, and his hands had felt big-boned in hers. She was forming a picture of a ruddy-cheeked, craggy-faced cowboy. She wondered if she was right. "I'm glad to meet you."

"Nice little gal you've got there."

"Holly, say hello to Mr. Rendell," Shanna prompted, but her daughter only drew back closer against her legs.

"Maybe Holly would like to try our fish pond sometime. We got trout leaping at a hook like popcorn out of a popper. Kids get a big kick out of it."

No response from Holly. Ariel was surprised that the little girl showed no interest in the man's offer. Usually Holly was open to any new activity, but now she just tugged at her mother's hand. "Come on, Mama."

"Got yourself a wait if yer aiming to see the doc," Ted said. "Waiting room's full."

Shanna almost turned heel and fled as he opened the door for her. The prospect of unseen curious eyes fastened on her sent a sickening plunge to the pit of her stomach.

"See ya later, Shanna," Ted said with a familiarity that she found a little presumptuous.

Like someone plunging into the dark unknown, she took a deep breath and walked into a room filled with the sound of shuffling feet, subdued voices, sporadic coughs and the plaintive crying of a infant. She had no idea where the reception desk was, but she had taken only a few steps inside the room when Marla's familiar voice came from her right.

"Hi, there. Dr. Jay said you might be dropping by, Shanna. We were kinda worried about you walking down the hill by yourself."

"No problem. I enjoyed the fresh air," Shanna countered with more enthusiasm than she felt.

"She stumbled a lot," said Holly with infuriating frankness. "And she wouldn't let me race down the hill with Ariel."

"Ariel?"

"Her little imaginary friend," said Shanna, wanting to sink into the floor. She was definitely going to have to have a talk with her daughter.

Marla laughed. "Well, I'm glad all *three* of you enjoyed the walk." She put a guiding hand on Shanna's arm. "Why don't you have this chair. Holly can sit at the little table and look at a book."

Shanna could tell from the way Holly was hugging her side that she didn't want to do what the nurse was suggesting. There must be other children in the waiting room staring at her. "Maybe later," Shanna said, and made room for Holly to share the chair with her.

Ariel snooped around the clinic and Marla's living quarters in the back and found nothing of interest. She knew that Ted Rendell had stopped in next door at the Timberline Bar. As Holly's guardian angel, Ariel never had any reason to be in such a place, but she knew that a lot of talking went on when people got to drinking. Maybe listening to local gossip wasn't a bad idea.

The dimly lit tavern boasted a western decor of mounted animal trophies, horseshoes, lariats and photos of grinning fishermen hold up strings of fish. Loud voices, the clatter of glasses and bottles, and a bellowing country tune created a raucous din that vibrated to the open-beam ceiling.

It seemed to Ariel that half the male population of the town was clustered at the bar or sitting in booths lining the knotty pine walls. The only two women she saw in the room were a broad-in-the-beam gal in tight jeans, dancing with a bean-pole of a partner in front of the jukebox, and Janet Rendell, who was sitting in a back booth with her husband.

As a potbellied waiter wearing a dirty apron set two bottles of beer in front of the Rendells, Ariel settled on the back of their booth above Janet's head, unabashedly listening to their conversation.

"The young doc seemed like a pleasant enough fellow. Gave me some sample ointment for my rash. Didn't talk much," Ted said. He took a big swig of beer and wiped the froth from his mouth with his sleeve. "I didn't learn any more about him than you did when you wrote your piece about him taking over for his dad."

"Marla says he can't wait to get back to the Big Apple. He hasn't shown any interest in staying in Colorado."

"Is Dr. Harrison Senior coming back?"

"Hard to tell. Marla's worried about him. If you ask me, she has more than just a professional interest in the good doctor. We're going into Denver this weekend to do some shopping, and she wants to stop by his house and see him." Jan's eyes narrowed. "I wonder if he knows his son is coming and going from Shanna Ryan's house all hours of the night and day?"

"The doc's car was parked out in front when I went out to the barn this morning to feed the horses," Ted told her. "And she was just going into his office as I was leaving. Maybe the reluctant doctor will be sticking around longer than we think. Can't say that I blame him. She's some tempting dish with that strawberry blond hair and—"

"Don't you get any ideas, buster," his wife snapped.

He looked shocked, but his smile was mocking. "Don't you believe in the good neighbor policy, my precious sweetheart?"

"Don't sweetheart me, you—" she broke off as Lew Walker shuffled over to their booth.

"Hope I'm not interrupting." He shuffled on his skinny bandy legs. "Was just by your place. Dropped off those tools you loaned me, Ted. Thanks."

"Sit down. Have a beer with us," Ted said as if relieved to have someone else to talk with.

"Well, I don't mind if I do." Lew slid in beside Ted, ignoring Janet's obvious glare.

Ted raised his hand and motioned to the waiter for three more beers. Then he asked Lew, "Did you get one of those junkers of yours going?"

"Naw. Need to buy some new parts. The old ones are all worn-out. Have to wait, though. Emma's death has left me a little short. Don't know if I'll like working for that niece of hers."

"Guess you're a little disappointed Emma didn't leave you a little something," Janet said with her usual deliberate bluntness. "I mean, you were friends, and all? You'd have thought the old gal would rather have you get the house than some relative who never showed her face around here."

"Reckon Emma did what she thought best."

"You think that gorgeous niece of hers is really going to stick around?" Ted ignored his wife's glare. "I can't see a gal like that planting her roots in an out-of-the-way place like this."

Janet glared at him. "I told you that she's aiming to make a B and B out of it."

Lew nodded. "That's what she's saying."

"Well, it's a damn shame, Lew. We could have made a good deal with you for that place," Janet said. "You wouldn't have to fix up old cars and be everybody's handyman if Emma had left the property to you."

"But she didn't. Emma never promised me nothing." He drew deeply on his beer, and then set the half-empty bottle down rather forcefully.

"Maybe Shanna Ryan will end up selling it, after all," Janet said with a straight face. "I mean, if her eyes don't get better, how she going to manage?"

"She told me her lack of vision was just temporary," Ted said. "That she wasn't really blind."

Neither Janet nor Lew said anything. Ted changed the subject. "I hear the highway department is finally going to smooth out some of the curves on Antler's Pass. You ought to look into it, Jan. Might make a good article."

Ariel listened for a few more minutes to their idle conversation, and then returned next door just as Jay came out into the waiting room to guide Shanna into the examination room.

"Shall we take a look at those eyes now?"

The smile that eased into her face mocked his professional tone. "Yes, Doctor."

Marla asked Holly if she'd like a glass of lemonade. Shanna was relieved when her daughter accepted. The nurse took her into her apartment while Jay led Shanna into the small examination room and reached for the ophthalmoscope.

As he eased her down in the chair, he lightly gave her shoulder a reassuring squeeze and she put her hand up to cover his. "Let's have a look."

She found she was holding her breath during the examination. When he was finished, he said in an encouraging tone. "No sign of more damage. And there's been some promising improvement."

"Thank heavens," Shanna breathed with relief.

"I'd say that things are looking good."

"But how long will it be till I can really see?"

"Your sight will come back slowly. The focus will gradually be sharper. The dark shadows will lighten. Have you noticed any difference between yesterday and today?"

"Maybe, slightly. I'm moving around the house better, but of course, thanks to you and Marla, I have things set out now and know where they are." She gave him that sweet, devastating grin of hers. "And I made it here without any problem."

Her innocence tore at his heart. Didn't she realize that her brave attitude could invite disaster? Especially now. Jay's frustrating visit with Skaggs had done little to ease his mind. If anything, he felt his apprehension growing as his mind skirted around unthinkable possibilities. He needed to talk to Shanna about his growing suspicion that the nut on the phone had been the one responsible for the jammed accelerator.

"I'll be through here in another half hour. Why don't you wait and let me drive you home? There are some things we need to talk about."

"Aren't you going back to Denver tonight?"

"I'm not sure. It depends . . ."

"On what?"

On whether you'll let me move in with you or not. He didn't know where the determination had come from, but it seemed to spring into his mind full blown.

Ariel nodded her approval as she caught his unspoken thought. The telepathic circuits between them were getting stronger all the time. If only she could tell Jay outright what she'd heard in the bar, but she couldn't. As a spiritual being she could appear, disappear and interact only if acceptance made it possible. With heavenly spirits all around them, adults were infuriatingly blind.

AFTER A QUICK SUPPER of scrambled eggs and ham, which Jay and Shanna prepared together in the big kitchen, he told her about his visit to Deputy Skaggs's office. "The man is so damn narrow-minded and provincial, he couldn't look at a situation with an open mind if his life depended on it."

"What about the telephone call?"

"He just shrugged it off. Outsiders aren't welcome in Westridge. Especially people who aim to change anything. He didn't see the call as a threat, just as a blunt invitation for you to leave."

"Maybe he's right."

No, he isn't. Ariel nearly sprouted wings just so she could flap them furiously. She wanted to materialize with a radiance of angelic magnificence and stun them with her presence, but she couldn't. She'd been warned about angel magic. She could help, but the people involved had to come to the truth themselves and deal with the situation in an earthly way. Sometimes she wished she could get their attention in a way they wouldn't forget.

"I'm concerned about your being here alone." Jay steeled himself for battle. As diplomatically as he could, he said, "Since you have all those empty bedrooms upstairs, why don't I spend at least tonight here? I can go back to Denver early in the morning and check on Dad."

Holly, who had been sitting on the sofa with them, clapped her hands. "Goodie, goodie, you can read to me. Mama can't read my new book. Do you like the Berenstain Bears?''

"Are they friendly bears?" he teased.

"Yes. Nice bears," Holly assured him as she leaped down and ran off to the kitchen to find her book.

Jay watched Shanna's face to see how she was taking his bold suggestion that he spend the night. He couldn't tell. Should he press his point or would that just raise her resistance to his suggestion? He decided to wait before saying anything more.

In truth, Shanna's emotions had never been pulled in so many directions at one time. Should she let him stay? His presence in the house would be a comfort, and if he wanted to sleep here instead of at his dad's place, why not? The offer hadn't been sexually motivated, she argued with herself.

Or had it?

What were his true feelings for her? Just compassionate concern? Or something more? She was in the dark in more ways than one. Just as bewildering was the way she felt about him. To her chagrin, she'd already invited his close embrace more than once, and her need to be with him went far beyond anything she'd experienced before. How could she trust her feelings, let alone his?

"I know what you're thinking," he said quietly.

"Do you?"

"I couldn't . . . and I wouldn't . . . take advantage of the situation."

"Not even if I wanted you to?"

He swallowed but managed to answer lightly, "Not even if you dragged me into bed with you."

"Well, that's plain enough." She caught her lip and started to get up from the sofa, but he pulled her back down beside him.

"Listen to me," he ordered in a gruff voice, his face just inches from hers. "I want you... want you more than I've ever wanted any woman. Every masculine hormone in my body fires when I touch you. You create utter devastation in me when you smile, lean into my arms—" his voice deepened to a groan "—and make me want to kiss you... like this!"

She wasn't prepared for the possessive capturing of her mouth by his. A spiraling heat radiated through her body, and a bewildering sensation drew her out of herself in a frightening way. The kiss went far beyond the fiery contact of their lips. Consumed by a hunger she'd never felt before, she clung to him, and when he withdrew his mouth, tenderly and slowly, she came reeling back down to earth with a gasp.

"Now, do you believe that I want to make love to you? And do you know why I can't?" He turned away so her soft, appealing lips wouldn't tempt him again. "You're fragile and vulnerable and caught in a situation of deep stress. This is not the time."

She opened her mouth to protest, but at that moment Holly came bounding back into the room and crawled up on his lap. While he read Holly the story, Shanna sat on the sofa bed beside them and tried to get her emotions back under sensible control. When Jay finished the story, he lightly kissed them both good-night, and even though Shanna had not said that he could stay, he went out to the car, brought in his overnight bag and and took himself upstairs.

He heard Shanna moving around below him for quite a long time. He could visualize her getting ready for bed. Brushing that gorgeous honey-red hair. Slipping on a soft, clinging nightgown that whispered as she moved. Settling her head upon the pillow and her long legs under the covers. The temptation to go back downstairs was fire in his veins. That one kiss had threatened to bend his willpower into a pretzel. He knew what would happen if he didn't keep the stairs and floor between them. He turned restlessly in the old-fashioned brass bed. What he needed was an ice-cold shower. Maybe two of them!

About an hour later, he had just slipped off to sleep when someone leaned on the doorbell and pounded loudly on the front door. Jiggs bounded out of the sitting room where Holly was sleeping. He raced down the hall so fast his paws slipped on the hardwood floor.

"Who in the—?" Jay grabbed his robe, shoved his feet into his slippers and hurried down the stairs. "Quiet, Jiggs," he ordered when he reached the front hall, but he knew the commotion would have already awakened Shanna.

He could see a man's form through the window, but Jay didn't recognize who it was until he opened the door. Ted Rendell stood there, hatless and coatless, and waved his arms in frantic gestures.

"Come quick, Doc. It's my wife. I...I think she might be dead."

"I'll be with you in a minute."

"What is it?" Shanna called from her bedroom doorway.

"An emergency. Nothing you can do. Go back to bed." Jay grabbed his jacket and the medical bag that he'd left in the hall. "I'll follow your car."

Maybe he should have taken time to put on some clothes, he thought as the cold night air whipped through his pajamas. He always slept in his clothes at the hospital and was used to being on his feet and ready to go in a split second after waking.

When they pulled up in front of the ranch house aglow with lights, Ted jerked open Jay's car door. "Hurry... hurry. She's in the barn."

"Barn?"

Ted explained in short, tight breaths. "I just got back from Cedarville. Didn't even go in the house. As soon as I got out of the car, I heard a horse thrashing and neighing in the stable. When I got there I saw that Jan's mare, Lady, was highly agitated. She was pawing something on the floor of the stall." Ted's voice broke. "I didn't see Jan at first. She was just lying there all bloody... not moving."

As they came into the stable, a dark horse looked up from the first stall, but the door hung open on the second stall. No horse there. Just Janet Rendell. She lay in a twisted position on the floor. Her bleached hair was matted with blood, her clothes torn and stained, and her glassy eyes stared at Jay as he knelt over her. He took her wrist and felt for a pulse. Her skin was slightly cool to the touch but not cold, he noted. Blood had stopped flowing from her wounds some time ago. Jay shook his head and he straightened up. "I'm so sorry."

"Oh, God." Ted turned and stumbled out of the stable. He leaned against the wall and gave in to deep, wrenching gasps.

Ariel had flashed to the barn ahead of the two men. Taking a sweeping look around, she noted a small tack room that contained all kinds of horse paraphernalia, several western saddles and horseshoeing equipment. Hay, straw and grain indicated that the Rendells took good care of the horses. She wondered what had happened to Lady and was pleased when Jay asked, "Where's the mare?"

"She bolted out of the stall when I opened it. Ran off, God knows where. I'll shoot the murderous beast when I find her."

Someone in authority had to be called. Jay knew that, but he had no idea what the procedure was in a place like Westridge. In the city, there was a competent police force and local coroner on the spot when something like this happened. He hated to call Marla at this time of night, but she would know how to handle things.

The two men went into the house and Jay made the call. "Marla, can you come over to the Rendells'? There's been an . . . an accident."

She was there in five minutes, looking as if she had just jerked the curlers out of her hair and thrown on her wrinkled nurse's uniform from the day before. She stared at him in disbelief. "I can't believe it. Jan and I were going shopping in Denver this weekend. What in heaven's name could have happened?"

She looked at Ted sitting on the couch with his head in his hands. She eased down beside him and looked ready to bombard him with questions. Instead, she asked in thick voice, "Ted, what can I do?" Then she repeated, "What can I do, Ted?"

Jay answered for him. "We have to notify someone."

Marla nodded. "Better notify Skaggs."

Ted nodded.

Marla got up and went to the phone. Jay listened to her end of the conversation and decided that Deputy Skaggs wasn't any more alert at night than he was in the daytime. Marla finally told him angrily that he had to get his pudgy body out of bed and get his butt over to the Rendells.

When Skaggs finally arrived, only Ted went with him to the barn. Both Jay and Marla waited in the living room. When the two men came back Skaggs plopped down in the closest easy chair. The officer showed more irritation than interest when Ted told him again how he'd found his wife and then gone after the doctor. Skaggs glared at Jay. "How is it that you were in Westridge, Doctor? You usually head back to Denver as fast as you can on Thursday evening."

"I decided to stay over." Jay offered no further explanation.

"And Ted knew your change of plans?"

"I saw the doctor's car parked in front of Emma's house," Ted said in a listless voice. "I was going to telephone, but I didn't know the number, so I drove up there."

Skaggs pointedly glanced at his watch and, with a smirk, asked, "Were you making a house call at Shanna Ryan's house, Doctor?"

Jay wanted to knock the smirk off his fat, leering face. Now the whole town would know he'd spent the night with Shanna, and her reputation would be shredded into gossipy bits.

Marla stepped in quickly in an attempt to defuse the situation. "We're worried about Mrs. Ryan managing alone in the house with her little girl, so Dr. Jay and I have decided to take turns staying with her."

Jay sent her a grateful look, but Skaggs just grunted.

"There'll be an autopsy, of course," Jay said.

Ted's head came up. His eyes widened. "I don't want her... cut up."

Marla sat down beside the bereaved man and took his hand. "Ted, it's the law. We have to verify cause of death."

"But it's obvious," he protested.

Maybe too obvious, thought Ariel. She had positioned herself in the living room so she could take in everything. She was a novice at this police work, but she wondered why Skaggs didn't ask the obvious questions. What was the victim doing in the barn in the dead of night? And why would her mare go berserk and stamp her to death?

Jay was asking himself the same questions. He wished he'd taken more time to look over her body. Had all of Janet Rendell's injuries been caused by horse hooves? If anybody but Skaggs had been in charge he would have gone back to the barn for a second look.

Ted brought out a bottle of whiskey, and Skaggs seemed more interested in watching Ted pour a couple of drinks than in making any inquiries about how and why the death had occurred.

"I never did like that mare. Told Jan when she bought Lady that she was too high-strung."

Skaggs nodded. "When we find her, we'll put her down."

"Not if I see her first," Ted said, downing his third shot. "I'm going to put a bullet right between her eyes."

He reached for the bottle and filled both his and Skaggs's glasses again. As if suddenly realizing he wasn't being a good host, he offered one to Jay.

"No, thanks," Jay said with a pointed look at Skaggs. The deputy just shrugged and took a deep swig of his whiskey and water.

"Where is Billie Jo?" Marla asked, frowning.

"She's spending the night with the Randolph girl. I guess we'd better call her," Ted said helplessly as if grief had sapped all his strength. "Would you, Marla...?"

"Sure. But I don't think we'd better break it to her over the phone."

He nodded. "Whatever you think best."

Marla went into the kitchen, made the call, and then came back. She sent an anxious glance at Jay.

Ted saw her frown. "Did you get her?"

"Billie Jo wasn't there. There were no plans for her to spend the night."

Ted swore, and color rushed into his strained face. "She's with that birdbrain Jasper." He got to his feet, swaying slightly as he bellowed, "I'll go over to his place and drag her home by the roots of her hair."

"Easy, Ted." Marla parked her stout frame in front of him. "Better find out first if that's where she is. Sit back down, and I'll do some calling."

He started to argue, and then the starch seemed to go out of him. He slumped down on the couch and Jay thought he was going to start crying. If the man hadn't been consuming all that alcohol, Jay would have suggested a sedative.

Marla went back to the kitchen and made a half-dozen calls with no success. While she was gone, Skaggs turned to Jay. "You can leave now, Doc. Don't need to keep you any longer. I'm sure you want to get back to..." His hesitation was a smirk. "To your duties."

Jay didn't rise to the insult. "You have a victim getting colder by the minute. And a death scene that requires an investigation. May I be so bold as to ask what you intend to do as an officer of the law in this situation?"

"Not that it's any of your business. But when I'm ready, I'll notify the sheriff's office. They'll send the coroner up here from Cedarville."

Good, thought Jay. Anybody on the scene would be an improvement over Skaggs. "I want to see the coroner's report on this," Jay told him.

"What for?" Skaggs's ruddy complexion deepened with a flash of anger.

"For my own satisfaction." Then Jay added pointedly as he started toward the door, "There are too many accidents around here to suit my taste."

Ariel clapped and silently cheered. Now they were getting somewhere. Jay returned to the house, but Ariel didn't go with him. She had something else on her mind.

Leaving the Rendell property, she made a sweeping detour over the hillside and up Clear Creek. Several times she picked up vibrations that led her to open pastures and ranches, but a skimming look at the livestock didn't turn up any sorrel mare.

Where had the animal gone?

She backtracked and nearly missed the animal. In the dark shadows of vaulting rocks, the mare was nearly invisible as it stood motionless in a deep crevice.

Easy girl. Easy.

With the softness of thistledown floating through the air, Ariel approached the sorrel mare. A warm sweat coated Lady's body and her hide quivered. Ariel alighted on her back, bent over and whispered in her ear. *It's all right, Lady.* Gently she urged the mare forward.

With guiding pressure on Lady's neck, Ariel guided her through the thick stands of conifers, over rocky terrain and down wooded slopes until they reached the sanctuary she hoped might save the animal's life.

"Here's some company for you, Johnny."

The black horse lifted his head and came trotting over to the gate. Ariel watched in satisfaction as the two horses slowly acknowledged the presence of the other and then softly moved together across the pasture.

Chapter Seven

When Shanna heard the front door open, she sat up, grabbed her robe, and without hesitation crossed the darkened room. She called in a whispered tone as she went out into the hall, "Jay?"

"Yes, it's me." He set down his doctor's bag, took off his jacket and went down the hall to meet her.

"What it is? Who's sick?"

Not sick. Dead. He didn't want to frighten her, but he knew that there was no way to keep the ugly death from her "It's Janet Rendell," he began, searching for the right words to explain her death. The whole thing was too bizarre to be believed. "Her husband found her in the barn. She'd been trampled to death by her riding mare."

Shanna's hand flew up to her face in horror, and she shivered. "Oh, no. How awful."

Jay slipped his arm around her waist. "Let me get you back to bed. There's nothing to be done tonight. The deputy and Marla are at the house with Ted. The coroner's been called."

"But how could such a thing happen? She must have been there a long time. I mean, it's the middle of the night."

"No. The body was still warm."

"But it's in the middle of the night."

"I know."

"Wasn't anybody home?"

"Ted was in Cedarville. He didn't say why. The daughter was supposedly spending the night with a girlfriend, but when we called, she wasn't there. Her father thinks Billie Jo's somewhere with her boyfriend."

Shanna debated about telling Jay what she knew about the two young people. Under normal circumstances, she would have kept quiet, but she felt the situation was too dire to keep silent. "I met both of them the day of my accident."

"You did? Where?"

Shanna told him about the two of them coming to the house. "I didn't know what they wanted, but I think I know now. Marla found a couple of their schoolbooks in one of the upstairs bedrooms. They must have been making use of the house while it was vacant."

Jay gave a low whistle. "Her father will really hit the roof if he hears about that. If I remember rightly I treated a Jasper Dietz once for a lacerated finger. He'd hurt himself in some automotive class. Not too bright as I recall. Anyway, I think Billie Jo is in for a rude awakening when she shows up in the morning."

"It's too awful. How did such a thing happen? Does anybody know?" Shanna asked as Jay helped her back into bed and tucked in the covers.

"Deputy Skaggs is looking into it," he lied. Then he sat down on the edge of the bed and took her hand. "I have to warn you that everybody in Westridge is going to believe we're sleeping together. Ted saw my car in front of the house and that's why he came here for me. I didn't take time to dress so I showed up in pajamas. Skaggs's smirk was as broad as his ugly face. I'm truly sorry. I should have known small-town gossip would jump to conclusions at a situation like this. Marla tried to cover for me, but I don't think anyone was fooled by her insistence that my presence in the house was strictly professional.''

''And is it?'' she challenged quietly.

''What do you think?'' he asked huskily, wanting to slip the tiny straps of her lace gown from her shoulders and bury his face in the sweet crevice of her breasts. No woman had ever offered such a temptation as she did with her hair spread out on the pillow like silken strands and her mouth softly curved in an inviting smile. Damn his well-trained conscience. Damn the deep-seated integrity that made him leave her bed with a curt, ''Get some sleep. Doctor's orders.''

She smiled softly to herself as she heard his restless footsteps pacing the floor above her. She felt contented and strangely loved even if he had rejected her gentle invitation to seduce him.

JAY AROSE EARLY the next morning, let Jiggs out and had coffee made when Holly padded into the kitchen clutching both her teddy and Bunny. Ariel floated in with her, glad to see that her sleuthing partner was in a good mood.

''Good morning,'' Jay said, smiling at Holly's tousled hair and pink cheeks. ''How'd you sleep?''

''With my eyes closed,'' she answered solemnly. Then she cocked her head. ''How do you sleep?''

He laughed "The same way." He lifted her up, and gave her a squeeze. "You're pretty smart, do you know that?"

"I'm five years old," Holly said, as if that explained everything.

"Then you can tell me what you'd like for breakfast," he invited as he opened a cupboard door.

She pointed to a box of Cheerios and a package of chocolate candy bars. "That and that."

"Whoa," he said with a suppressed chuckle. "Candy bars?"

She shrugged her tiny shoulders as if anything was worth a try.

Ariel watched the two of them with amusement. If the handsome doctor stayed around Holly very long, he'd learn a lot about kids that wasn't in any medical journal.

An hour later, Shanna came into the kitchen dressed in bright crimson shorts and matching sleeveless top. Thanks to Marla's safety pins, she had matched the outfit correctly. She had gathered her ringlets back in a gold clip and touched a pale shade of ruby gloss to her lips. She felt deliciously feminine and in need of masculine approval.

No one was in the kitchen. When she heard voices outside, she made her way to the back door. Jay's deep laughter was mingled with her daughter's high-pitched giggles. "What's going on out here?" Shanna demanded as she stepped out into the sunshine.

Jay was conscious of a compelling radiance about her that stunned him. Sunlight burnished her curly hair with golden red brilliance, and the impact of her supple, lithe body in shorts nearly stopped the rhythm of his heartbeat. He'd never seen a woman more desirable in his life. The palms of his hands were suddenly moist, and he felt an ache building with demanding force.

"Hello?" she said, puzzled by his silence. "Are you there?"

He fought for a normal tone. "We're just coming back from a hike up the hill. Your daughter's a great little climber." *And you're breathtakingly beautiful.*

Holly ran to her mother. "I got up on a rock this big." She held her hands out in a wide gesture.

Shanna's breath caught as her eyes relayed a distinct image of Holly's tiny figure and the movement of her arms. Her sight was coming back!

"Why are you crying, Mama?"

"What is it?" Jay was instantly at Shanna's side.

She brushed away the fullness in her eyes and squinted at his face. She couldn't see his features distinctly, but the lines and planes of nose, mouth and cheeks were identifiable. "I can almost see you."

"Hallelujah!" He lifted her up by the waist and twirled her around. She laughed as tears of happiness flowed down her cheeks.

Holly and Ariel looked at each other, clapped their hands, and then began dancing around the couple, laughing and singing, "She can see. She can see."

Jay set Shanna down and was about to kiss her when their jubilation was cut short by the sound of heavy footsteps coming around the corner of the house. Skaggs's gruff voice demanded, "What's going on here? I've been lying on the doorbell for ten minutes."

"We're celebrating. To what do we owe this early-morning visit?" Jay asked without any welcome in his voice.

"I've got something that belongs to Mrs. Ryan. Found it behind a bale of hay in the Rendell barn."

Even in the bright sunlight, Shanna felt a penetrating chill. She could barely make out that he was holding something rectangular. "What is it?"

"A photo album. Yours."

"But that's impossible."

"Let me see that." Jay reached for the album, but Skaggs drew it back.

"This is official business," Skaggs snapped. "And it sure ain't any of yours, Doctor."

"I'm making it my business. Now, what makes you think that belongs to Mrs. Ryan?"

"Got her name on it. See there." He pointed to gold script letters, The Ryans, imprinted on the cover. "It's hers all right. Plenty of pictures inside of the happy family. Now, what I'm aiming to know is what this here picture book was doing near the stall where Janet Rendell was stomped to death?"

"I...I don't know," stammered Shanna. The whole thing was too absurd. She couldn't even remember the last time she'd seen the album. Probably when she packed all their personal stuff for the movers, she thought. She was positive she hadn't unpacked it in the few days they'd been in Aunt Emma's house.

"Did you give it to Mrs. Rendell?"

"No, of course not. The woman only came to the house once. The day of my accident. We only talked for a few minutes, and I certainly didn't hand over my photo album to her."

"Think, Shanna," Jay urged quietly. "Could she have picked it up without your knowing it? Maybe slipped it out of the house somehow?"

"I don't see how." Shanna tried to remember everything that had gone on during Janet's visit. "I let her in. We went into the sitting room and talked. Then she left."

"Could she have picked up the album from the sitting room and slipped it out? Sounds like the kind of thing she might do to get more intimate details for her article."

"I'm positive that the album hadn't been unpacked yet."

"It must have," he insisted.

Skaggs swore, "Dammit, you back off, Doctor. I'm the one asking questions here."

Jay's expression hardened. "I don't intend to stand by and let you badger her. As her physician—"

"And more than that, I'll wager," Skaggs said snidely. "I wasn't born yesterday, but that's neither here nor there. I want Mrs. Ryan to look through the book—"

"But I can't," protested Shanna. "I don't see well enough to know what I'm looking at."

"You sure as hell should be able to tell if she took any pictures out of it."

Shanna frowned. It had been such a long time since she'd looked at the album that she couldn't remember exactly what photos she'd put in it. She'd bought the book when she was pregnant with Holly so they'd have a place for baby pictures. She'd added other photos as time went on, but she didn't remember exactly which ones. "I know that the last snapshots I put in that book were Holly's third birthday because those photos filled all the pages of that album. I can't imagine that Janet or anyone else would find my family snapshots of interest. As for her stealing the album, it's ridiculous.''

"Then you must have given it to her," snapped Skaggs.

"I didn't."

"Then when did she get it?"

The night she was in the house. Ariel was so excited she almost gave a burst of luminosity that would have blinded everyone there. It must have been Jan Rendell who had left her lingering aura in the house.

Shanna's thoughts must have been going in the same direction. "The other night, Jiggs raised a fuss and I found the door unlocked," she said thoughtfully. "I guess she could have been in the house." If her daughter and boyfriend had been letting themselves in and out with a key, Janet could have gotten hold of it, too.

"But would Janet Rendell think a photo album important enough to become a housebreaker?" countered Jay.

Skaggs snorted. "Of all the tomfoolery! You expect me to believe that Jan burglarized your house to steal a photo album?"

"If Shanna didn't give her the album, then she must have taken it from the house at some time...either the day she talked with Shanna or at another time," Jay reasoned, doing the deputy's thinking for him.

"All right, Doctor," Skaggs said with sarcastic emphasis. "Tell me why she'd want the damn thing?"

"Maybe she thought there was something in it that would make a good story." The explanation sounded too thin even to Jay.

"Oh, really? Is that why two pages are torn out of it?"

"What?" Shanna gasped.

"You can see the rough edges." Skaggs opened the album and held it out to her so she could let her fingers play over the jagged remains.

Anger started in the pit of Shanna's stomach and found its way into her voice. "How dare she!" The mutilation was a personal assault. The first years of Holly's life were chronicled in those snapshots. Fury made her lips tremble. "Those pictures were precious to me. I want them back."

"Well, now, that ain't going to be easy unless you give me something to go on.

"Did you search the house for the missing pages?" Jay demanded.

"How'd I know they were missing? Mrs. Ryan could have torn out the pages herself."

"Well, I didn't," Shanna answered quickly. "I don't know what's going on here, but I'll tell you one thing. Janet Rendell took my album without my permission, and that's all I know. I have no idea why it ended up in her barn. When you find out why, I would most certainly like to know." A flush of anger reddened her fair cheeks. "Now, if you'll excuse me, Deputy Skaggs, it's time for breakfast."

"I already ate," piped up Holly as she emptied a sand pail she'd been filling. She jumped up, took her mother's hand and sent Jay a smug look as she added, "But I didn't have dessert."

Shanna couldn't help laughing as the two of them went into the house. Ariel lingered outside with Jay and Deputy Skaggs. She was worried that someone might have reported the whereabouts of the sorrel mare. If Ted Rendell knew where Lady was, he might drive to Deerview with a loaded gun and carry out his promise to shoot the horse between the eyes.

"Has Billie Jo shown up yet?" asked Jay. Somehow he was more inclined to think Jan's daughter and her boyfriend might have lifted the album from the house. For what reason, he couldn't imagine, but a firm conviction was building that Shanna's photo album had drawn her into some macabre situation that put her in immediate danger.

"Nope. The Dietz kid isn't home, either. The two of them must be shacking up somewhere. This isn't the first time they've run off together. They've been disappearing off and on all year. They hole up somewhere for a couple of days and then show up as if nothing's the matter. The last few times I wasted my time looking for 'em. Never did find them."

Did you check Emma's empty house? thought Jay. From what Shanna had told him about the schoolbooks, he'd bet that's where the runaway teenagers had been holed up.

"Short of locking the two of them up, there ain't much their folks can do about it. Billie Jo's going to get a kick in the rear this time, though. Her dad's pretty strung out."

"Why don't you ask Billie Jo about the album?"

"What in the hell would she know about that?"

"I don't know, but maybe you'd find out if you asked her."

"Don't tell me how to do my job."

Somebody should, thought Jay as Skaggs turned around and stomped away.

When Jay went back into the house, Shanna was just sitting down with a cup of coffee and some fresh toast. "I really can see better," she told him with a joyful lift of her chin. "Not very clearly, but a lot better than yesterday."

"Listen. Why don't we take a ride and I'll show you my dad's place."

"You're not going back to Denver today?"

"Not until later. And I'm not scheduled at the clinic, so my time's my own. How about it, Holly, would you like to see Johnny, my dad's horse?"

"Will you take me for a ride?"

He shook his head. "Afraid not. I don't know much about riding." He looked at Shanna. "Do you like horses?"

"I've never been around them."

"Well, you'll like Johnny. My dad's made a pet out of him. He'll nudge and nuzzle you until you pet him or give him something to eat."

"Does he like candy bars?" asked Holly, still working on getting one for herself.

"Sorry, Holly, no candy bars for you *or* Johnny," her mother said.

As Shanna and Jay laughed together, a wonderful warm aura circled around them. Ariel beamed. Love was pure magic sometimes.

"How about it? Will you and Holly spend the day with me? You'll like Deerview. We could have a picnic."

Holly clapped her hands. "I like picnics. Can I invite Ariel?"

Jay and Shanna exchanged amused glances. "Why not," he said. "The more the merrier."

Jay was relieved. Now he could keep Shanna safely with him most of the day. He felt guilty about leaving his dad alone for a third night. Since Marla had offered to take turns staying with Shanna, Jay was wondering how he could get Shanna to accept the offer. He didn't want to leave Westridge without having arranged for someone to keep her company. She'd probably kick up a fuss if she thought someone was baby-sitting her.

The drive from Westridge to Deerview was on a narrow road that followed Miners Creek through a narrow canyon and then dropped down into a natural park of spring green meadows. Jay described the changing scenery to Shanna as best he could. He rolled down the window so she could hear the sound of rushing water flowing over rocks and along mossy tree-lined banks.

"Why do they call it Miners Creek?"

"According to my dad, in the 1800s there was a lot of panning for gold in this area. I guess prospectors were all over the place trying to strike it rich. You can still see mine tailings high on the mountainsides and the remains of an old mill built on the creek, but that's about all that's left of those days. My dad will talk your ear off about early Colorado history. I think he's sorry he was born a hundred years too late."

She smiled. "I'd like to get to know him."

"You'll like him. He's a great guy." Jay frowned. "Both of us have been so busy with our careers that we haven't spent a lot of time together these last few years."

Shanna was startled by the edge of loneliness in his voice. It sounded as though he, like herself with Aunt Emma, had gotten caught up in his own life and not made time to be with those he loved. Sadly, it had to be a heart operation that had brought Jay to Colorado for a visit.

Ariel had flashed ahead to Deerview and found Lady grazing contentedly beside Johnny. *What would Jay do when he found an extra horse in the pasture?*

At the sound of the approaching car, Johnny came trotting over to the fence. The sorrel mare lifted her head, watched the black horse stick his head over the fence, and then slowly followed him.

"You have *two* horses," Holly said excitedly as the pasture came into view.

"Well, I'll be," Jay said. "So I have."

Shanna could not see the two large animals distinctly, but she knew from Jay's tone that something was wrong. "What is it?" she asked as he braked to a stop.

"Johnny has company. A sorrel mare."

"Sorrel mare? Do you think it's Janet's Lady?"

"I'd bet on it. Ted said he opened the stall gate when he found his wife and the mare ran off. But how did she get into my pasture?"

"What are you going to do?" Shanna asked as they got out of the car.

"I don't know."

Holly had brought some carrots because they were the only thing in the refrigerator that Jay thought Johnny might like. As they walked over to the fence, Shanna wished she could she could see Jay's expression.

"Will he bite me?" Holly asked anxiously as Johnny stretched his neck to reached the carrot in her hand.

"Hold it like this," Jay instructed, putting a carrot in his open palm so that the horse could scoop it up with his foraging lips.

Holly did as she was told and let the horse's slobbering mouth suck the carrot out of her hand. "He likes it," she squealed excitedly as the horse chomped away.

Jay held out a carrot to the mare. "Here, Lady."

"What if she goes crazy again?" Shanna asked, keeping close to Holly.

As the mare moved cautiously but calmly closer, nothing about her indicated to Jay that she had trampled her mistress to death the night before. When she came close enough to hang her head over the fence, Jay fed her the carrot and looked her over from head to tail. She was sleek, graceful and a beautiful animal.

And a killer?

Jay stroked Lady's head with his free hand. "She seems docile enough. Her eyes are soft and gentle. I can't imagine what made her agitated enough to trample Janet Rendell to death. Unless—"

"Unless what?"

"I think we should call a vet and have him draw some blood. If Skaggs was worth his salt, he would have told Ted that the horse couldn't be destroyed until he made some tests."

"Do you think she might have been given something?"

"Easy, girl," he soothed the mare as his fingers lifted her mane in a stroking gesture. She flinched at his touch. He gently pushed the silky strands of her mane to one side. "What in the—"

"What is it?"

"I'll be damned. There are some small sores under her mane. As if she's been burned with something round and hot."

Chapter Eight

Jay examined the sores closely. "Looks as if she's been burned with something sharp. Whatever it was went quite deep."

"How awful," Shanna said, feeling sick to her stomach.

"One more reason to have a vet look her over," Jay said grimly. After a moment, he asked, "How would you like to take a ride over to Cedarville? I think this should be reported to someone in the sheriff's office. Skaggs will be fighting mad about me going to his superior, but someone with a brain in his head should be very interested in these neck burns. I don't know how the mare showed up in our pasture, but I'm glad she did."

Ariel was more pleased than ever that she had secreted the horse away. If anybody else had found Lady, they would have probably returned her to her owner and allowed Ted to carry out his threat to shoot her on sight. This new evidence that the horse had been injured might be important, and she was glad that Jay was going to look into it. Although she'd been lucky so far, trying to get mortals to follow through on things wasn't as easy as she had imagined. They certainly all had minds of their own.

On the drive to the county seat, Shanna and Jay smiled at each other as they heard Holly chatting away in the back seat with her imaginary friend. No doubt about it, thought Jay, the little girl was certainly creative. The one-way conversation seemed to make perfect sense to Holly as she laughed and pointed out the window.

Cedarville was about an hour and a half drive west into the Colorado Rockies. The picturesque mountain town lay in a valley caught between green wooded hillsides and snow-capped peaks. Jay smiled at a sign at the outskirts bragging of a population of 9,420 residents. Jay noticed that houses and businesses showed evidence of a healthy economy, unlike Westridge. This would have been a better place for Shanna's B and B. Too bad her aunt Emma hadn't left her a Victorian house in Cedarville.

"There's a park," squealed Holly. "Let's stop, Mama. Please, Mama."

"Do you want to stop here and wait for me while I talk to the sheriff?" Jay asked.

Shanna knew how much Holly liked to play on swings and merry-go-rounds, but the idea of not being able to supervise her daughter properly frightened her. Even though her sight was slightly improved, the view out the car window still resembled a blurred, faded piece of film. She'd heard too many horror stories of children being snatched in playgrounds. Maybe she was getting paranoid, but until her sight returned she wasn't going to take any chances. She shook her head. "Not now, Holly."

Jay stayed the child's tearful protest with a promise. "Tell you what, Holly, if it's all right with your mother, as soon as we take care of business, we'll pay a visit to the park."

"Goody." Holly clapped her hands. "Will you push me high, high, in the swing like Ariel does?"

"You betcha."

Shanna sent him a grateful look. Her husband had never liked going to public parks and playgrounds.

Helpful signs guided them to the county courthouse. As he parked in front of the old stone building, he turned to Shanna. "I think it would be better if you didn't go in with me."

"Why not?"

"I don't want anybody to start grilling you. My main concern is getting that mare looked at."

"Are you going to tell them about the photo album?"

"I'll let Skaggs put it in his report. At the moment, I just want somebody besides Skaggs to be brought in on the investigation. And if that isn't possible, I can at least bring some pressure from his superiors to make him check out every bit of evidence he's likely to miss." He silently determined that he'd tell them about the threatening telephone call and the possibility that Shanna's car had been tampered with by the same person.

"There's a small coffee shop across the street." Jay looked at his watch. "Almost lunchtime. Why don't I walk you and Holly to the café and you can wait for me there?"

"How long do you think you'll be?" Shanna asked, trying to decide if she preferred to stay in the car rather than manage by herself in a strange place.

"I really don't know. It depends." He thought about his recent visit to Skaggs's office. "I'm hoping to get some quick action, but who knows?" He wished he was dealing with an urban law enforcement agency instead of a county sheriff and his scattered deputies.

"What about the picnic?" Holly reminded them with childlike tenacity.

"Right you are," agreed Jay. "Why don't you two order some lunches to go while I go see the sheriff?"

Shanna put aside her apprehension and agreed. Jay ordered from the menu and left them enjoying a couple of soft drinks.

With Ariel moving along unseen beside him, Jay hurried back across the street and entered the small building housing all the county offices and county jail.

A plain, bespectacled young woman with a pencil stuck behind her ear sat behind a reception counter in the outer office.

Ariel, hovering at Jay's side, wanted to laugh at the woman's wide-eyed stare when she looked up and saw Jay standing there. Jay's dark hair was slightly tousled on his forehead, and in his light blue slacks and sportshirt, he could have passed for a magazine model advertising the latest in men's sportswear. "Can I help you?" she asked in a tone of wonderment.

"I hope so." Jay handed her his business card and told her he would like to see the sheriff.

Holding the card in her hand, she peered through the thick lenses at his name, title and address. Obviously a handsome city doctor was not a routine visitor to the Cedarville courthouse. "New York?" she said with the same kind of disbelief she might have said, *Mars?*

He nodded, and added, "At the moment, I'm staying in Westridge. Helping out in the clinic there. It's important that I talk with the sheriff as soon as possible."

"I'm sorry. Sheriff Dunbar is out of town."

"Then, I'd like to speak with the law officer in charge."

"Deputy Withers?"

"If he's the officer in charge. Yes."

She pointed down the hall. "Second door on your right."

"Thank you." Jay gave her a melting smile that brought a flush of embarrassment to her face. For a moment, Ariel thought the poor woman was going to faint from the warmth of his masculine attention.

Jay's footsteps echoed on the polished floors, and muffled voices floated out into the nearly deserted hall as he passed some closed doors. I guess this is what you call a low-key government, he thought as he compared the quiet serenity with the cacophony of Manhattan's frantic public buildings. The contrast worried him. Did anything ever get done in these mountain communities?

Jay geared himself to face some disgruntled, uncooperative officer like Skaggs, and was set for a confrontation as he stiffened his shoulders and knocked on the door.

"It's open."

An older man sitting behind a desk looked up as Jay came into the small office. He lifted a graying eyebrow, and his lips curved in a smile. "Can I help you?"

"Deputy Withers?" Jay inquired.

"That's me." The rangy, easy-moving officer stood up and offered his hand for a shake. "And you are—?" Jay introduced himself and the man nodded. "Have a seat, Doctor. What can I do for you?"

Ariel had swooshed down in the chair next to Jay's and decided she liked the look in the man's eyes. You could always tell a lot by a mortal's eyes. Sometimes you could see right into their honest souls. This man wasn't like Deputy Skaggs. Deputy Withers listened attentively to what Jay had to say, nodding now and then.

Yes, he'd heard about the Rendell woman's unfortunate accident and the coroner's midnight trip to Westridge, he told Jay. "I'm a horse lover myself, but they can be unpredictable as hell, sometimes. Something must have spooked the mare."

When Jay told him what he had discovered under the horse's mane, Withers leaned forward, the lines in his long, lean face deepening. "Have you told Deputy Skaggs about this?"

"No, I came directly here after I found the burns under the horse's mane. Why didn't I go to Skaggs?" Jay said before the officer could ask. "Because I find Skaggs to be incompetent, prejudiced and intellectually dense. In short, I find the deputy totally incapable of handling and preserving evidence."

Jay waited, and when Withers didn't defend Skaggs, the officer's silence told Jay a lot. "I don't want anything to slip through his hands—like making sure that a complete autopsy is performed on Janet Rendell. I came here to make sure her horse is examined by an expert and a blood sample taken for analysis."

Hurrah! Ariel clapped a hand over her mouth, fearful that she might have voiced the cheer aloud.

The men seemed oblivious to her presence, so she guessed the cheer had gone unnoticed. She wished oral communication wasn't so slow. Telepathic exchanges were so much more efficient. She sighed. Maybe someday mortals would be more open to ESP.

Deputy Withers laced his long, slender fingers together, looked at Jay for a long minute, and then asked quietly, "What else is on your mind?"

Jay was grateful that the officer was perceptive enough to know that there was more than just the horse's condition that had brought him here. He hardly knew where to start.

The telephone call, prompted Ariel.

Much to her delight, Jay leaned forward and said, "Yesterday, Shanna Ryan, who recently moved to Westridge, received a threatening telephone call while I was at her house. And it's the wording of the threat that worries me."

"What was the threat?"

" 'Leave Westridge. Or your next accident will kill you.' Some nut could just be taking advantage of the fact that she had a bad car accident recently, but maybe 'next' means he had something to do with the 'first.' And if he did—"

Withers cut him off with a wave of his hand. "I remember the accident. The office was talking about it when the report came in. Took a curve too fast and—"

"Because the accelerator stuck."

"Yes, that's what she said, but it could be she didn't want to fess up to driving over the speed limit."

"Shanna isn't the kind to lie about anything, I know that now. I'll admit I thought the same thing at first, but there are too many unanswered questions. If the car hadn't exploded, there might be some evidence that it had been tampered with.''

"True. There's little chance to verify a malfunction when all we've got is charred remains.''

"What if Shanna and her little girl were almost killed because someone arranged for her car to malfunction and go off the road? I think someone is determined to get rid of newcomers by one means or another. When you look at Janet Rendell's death—''

Withers cut him off with a wave of his hand. "You're talking like a man who thinks murder has been done. I'm sorry, Dr. Harrison, but I find it unreasonable to think that anyone is trying to control population by arranging car accidents and getting newcomers trampled to death by their horses.''

Ariel sent a whispered thought into Jay's ears. He weighed an idea for a moment, and then said, "Maybe controlling the population isn't behind the acts. Maybe it's something else.'' He'd hadn't the foggiest idea what that "something else" might be.

"Mrs. Ryan runs her car off a mountain road, receives a call telling her to leave Westridge, and Janet Rendell gets trampled to death by her horse. I fail to see what ties the three incidents together?''

"If I had all the answers I wouldn't be here,'' Jay answered impatiently. "I want the authorities to look into the situation. I don't know the politics involved nor who has jurisdiction over what, but I don't intend to let this matter rest in Deputy Skaggs's incompetent hands.''

Withers was silent for a moment. Then he nodded. "I tell you what I'll do. I'll give Sheriff Dunbar a call at the Denver hotel, lay the whole thing out for him and get his orders on what to do.''

"How long will that take?"

A faint smile played at the corners of the man's lips. "We can get our spurs spinning when we've a mind to, Doctor. Now, tell me where your place is located so we can have someone pick up the horse."

Jay gave him the information and also his father's Denver telephone and address. "I want to be kept informed."

Deputy Withers stood and held out his hand to shake Jay's. "Thanks for coming in, Doctor. We'll see what we can do and let you know what turns up."

Jay left the courthouse with Ariel moving along at his side. Unknowinlgly, he shared her satisfaction. Deputy Withers seemed like a competent officer who would make certain Sheriff Dunbar heard about Jay's visit. Good, she thought. Now she had a team of sleuths working with her. Angelo would be pleased about that. She liked her new role, but she wished there was a more poetic name for a gumshoe.

"Everything's taken care of," Jay told Shanna in a reassuring voice. "Now, Holly, lets find that park again." He paid for the order of food to go and took Shanna's arm, well aware of the admiring glances that came her way. She was a knockout in her crimson shorts, worth more than a second glance from any full-blooded male. As she walked beside him, her legs and hips moved with tantalizing grace. He wanted to put his arm around her waist in a possessive gesture for all the world to see.

Even though Jay was cheerful and kept the conversation light and entertaining as they drove back to the park, Shanna had the feeling that he was covering up some unspoken anxiety. He didn't refuse to answer her questions, but neither did he offer any details about his conversation with Deputy Withers. As they sat on the grass and ate their lunch of sandwiches and chocolate éclairs, he seemed content to interact with Holly, laughing with her at the antics of a ground squirrel who had invited himself to the festivities.

In the bright sunlight, there was more gray shading and fewer black images in Shanna's vision, but even this improvement didn't bring anything into clear focus. She could hear the creaks and groans of playground equipment and the happy din of children playing there, but she would have been lost if she'd tried to move around the playground. Thank heavens Jay was there to look after Holly, who gobbled down her food and begged to try out everything on the playground.

"All right, kiddo," Jay said as he gave in to her coaxing. "Let's give this place a good going-over."

"Behave yourself, Holly," Shanna admonished.

"You, too," teased Jay as he impulsively gave Shanna a light kiss. "Don't run away."

They left her sitting on the grass, and she leaned back on her arms, content to let her skin soak in the warm, tanning sun rays. As every muscle in her body relaxed, she lay back on the grass and closed her eyes.

Jay kept his eye on her while playing with Holly, and was pleased when he saw her stretched out on the ground, soaking up the sun. Good. She needed to relax, get out from under some of the stress.

Shanna didn't realized she'd fallen asleep until she came awake with a scream caught in her throat. She sat up, trembling with a hot sweat encasing her body.

She'd been dreaming. A horrible nightmare. Fleeing blindly in swirling blackness. Evil stalking her every step. Trapped. Clutching fingers reaching out for her—!

"No...no," she gasped, burying her face in her hands as she tried to control the shivers traveling up her spine.

Jay saw her jerk up with a cry and a panicked expression on her face. He left Holly circling on the merry-go-round and ran across the lawn.

"I'm here. It's all right." He drew her into the circle of his arms and tightened them protectively around her. "Don't be frightened. You're all right."

She pressed her cheek against his, breathing in the familiar scent of his hair as her fingers laced through the thick strands at the back of his neck.

"What happened?" he asked anxiously. "What frightened you?"

"Someone was stalking me...in the dark...I couldn't see."

"Just a bad dream," he assured her even as his own chest tightened. Her near-blindness was challenge enough, and he worried about the impact of all the other things that were happening in her life. No wonder she was having nightmares. How much could her courageous spirit take?

THEY RETURNED to Westridge about dusk. As Jay drove past the Rendell property, he saw several vehicles parked in front of the house and Ted talking to Lew Walker on the front porch, but neither of the men returned Jay's wave. In fact, the bandy-legged handyman glared at the car as if driving up the road to Shanna's house was some kind of trespassing.

On the way home, Jay had decided to phone Marla and ask her to stay the night while he returned to

Denver to check on his father and pick up a change of clothes. He'd drive back tomorrow and stay close for a few days until he was reassured that Sheriff Dunbar had taken charge of the situation.

Almost immediately, he had to make a change of plans. When he called the clinic, he got Marla's recorded message. "Sorry. Not here. Dentist appointment in Denver. Please call 9-1-1 in case of emergency."

"It's all right," Shanna assured him. "Holly and I will turn in early. There's no reason to think you have to baby-sit us."

"You're probably right, but I'm not going to leave town until I'm sure someone is close by in case you need help." He dialed Skaggs's office and got a recorded message telling a number to call in case of emergency. He called it.

Skaggs had his mouth full when he answered, and then swore when Jay explained what he wanted. "Surveillance? Where in the hell do you think you are? We ain't city folks with officers sitting around on their rumps watching houses. It's bad enough you went pussy-footing over to Cedarville behind my back."

"So you heard from Sheriff Dunbar?" Good, thought Jay. That probably meant somebody had picked up the mare.

"Sounds like you were spouting off pretty good, Doctor. Never mentioned your sweetie's album, though, did ya?"

Jay felt a coil tightening in the pit of his stomach. He knew he couldn't protect Shanna from the questioning that was certain to come since the blasted album tied her to the scene of Janet's death. There had to be some simple, benign explanation, but in the meantime, he hated to see her involved in the ugliness. That's all Shanna needed, he thought angrily as he answered, "I have confidence that Sheriff Dunbar will find out how Janet got hold of it. Anyway, I have to go back to Denver tonight, and I wanted you to know that Mrs. Ryan is going to be alone."

"What's the matter, Doctor. Is the little love nest breaking up?"

Jay wished he could flatten the deputy's bulbous nose all over his fat face, and it was all he could do to reply evenly, "If Mrs. Ryan calls you for help, you'd better get your butt over here or I'll have your badge. Is that clear?"

"Yes, sirree," Skaggs answered in a mocking tone.

Jay hung up with a punctuating slam. Damn. The man was an imbecile. He still had his hand on the phone when it rang. *Maybe Marla had changed her mind and not stayed over?* He eagerly lifted it, and was startled to hear his father on the other end of the line.

"Is something wrong, Dad?" He had given his father Shanna's number and told him he'd be at her house if he wasn't at the cabin.

"I was just wondering when you'd be home. It's getting kinda late." There was a wistful loneliness in the older man's voice that grabbed at Jay. "I let the nurse go tonight because you said—" His voice trailed off.

"I'm sorry, Dad. I didn't get away as soon as I had expected. Had to make a trip to Cedarville today. Just got back to Westridge. I'll tell you all about it when I get there. I'll be leaving in a few minutes," he promised. "But don't wait up for me."

"I'll be awake. Nights are mighty long when you don't feel like sleeping. Be careful on the road, son."

"I will. See you in a couple of hours."

Reluctantly, Jay went back into the kitchen where Shanna was putting out some cold cuts and cheese for dinner. He came up behind her, put his arms around her waist and let his face nuzzle the cleft of her neck and shoulders. "Hmm, nice."

She stiffened for a moment, and then let herself ease back against him in a warm, vibrant surrender that sent his pulse racing. Instinctively, his hands pressed her even tighter against his pulsating body and the hardening of his desire.

She groaned softly, and he knew that she was responding to his hunger with an ache of her own. If the situation had been different—but it wasn't, an ethical, uncompromising inner voice warned him. Nothing he could say or do would justify taking advantage of her present emotional state. He let his hands slip down the smooth curve of her hips, and then he abruptly dropped them to his side and stepped back.

She turned around slowly. Last night she'd had to fight with herself to let him stay because she'd viewed his insistence to spend the night as baby-sitting. Now every sensory bud in her body was firing with the need to be with him, to spend the night in his arms.

"I have to go back to Denver," he said as if the longing had been clear in her face.

"Oh . . . of course," she said with dry lips.

"I don't want to go, but I have to see to my father."

"I understand."

"Marla's not in town or I'd ask her to come and stay with you. But I've called Skaggs. He knows you're going to be alone. And if you get frightened for any reason, call 9-1-1. I'll be back tomorrow—"

"There's no need for that," she said quickly. She couldn't stand it if she became a burden to him. His caring tenderness was not something she should take for granted—or expect. She would hate herself if she became a weight around his neck. "I really need to have a little time to myself."

He didn't answer, and she wished once again she could see his expression. She had to guess whether or not he'd taken her words at face value. She let her hand rove up to his face, trailing her fingers along his cheek and the soft shock of hair that almost drifted over his eye. "Is your hair always so flyaway?"

He chuckled. "Always. When I was a teenager I tried to plaster it down, but I learned that nothing was going to tame it, so I just let it go."

She threaded her fingers through the thick waves. "I like it."

"I'm glad. I hope you feel the same way when you can really see me." He lowered her hand from his face because he couldn't trust himself to stand there any longer without sweeping her into a demanding embrace. "I'll be leaving now."

"Will you be back in the morning?"

"I'll try." He kissed her lightly on her forehead and turned away before her nearness wiped out the last ounce of his self-control.

She thought of a dozen things she should have said after he'd driven away and left her staring at the disappearing pinpoints of light in the encroaching darkness.

AFTER TUCKING HOLLY in bed, Shanna went to the back door and called Jiggs in for the night.

He didn't come.

Shanna waited another few minutes while she readied herself for bed, and then for the second time she went to the back door and called impatiently, "Jiggs! Come here."

Still no dog. Looking out into possessive shadows that obscured the slope of the hill, she couldn't see any movement that might be a dog running toward the house. As she stood there in the doorway, a hushed stillness reached her. Her lack of vision caused ghoulish images to shift before her eyes. Needled tree branches like skeleton fingers stabbed an indistinct night sky. Sensations like those in her nightmare made her step back into the house and quickly lock the door.

The blasted dog could stay outside all night, she told herself as she felt her way back to her bedroom and the security of her bed. But she couldn't relax. Jiggs was a beloved member of the family. He'd never disappeared like this before. Maybe he was just getting some exercise because he'd been shut up during their trip to Cedarville. He might have wandered farther away from the house than usual. Finally she convinced herself that he would be whining at the door in the morning, begging to get in.

Ariel had taken a quick look around when Jiggs had failed to answer Shanna's call. She'd always had a close affinity with Jiggs, and more than once she'd used a high-pitched sound to get his attention. She tried to call him in this fashion, but with no luck. The dog wasn't anywhere close to the house. Ariel knew that Holly would be heartbroken if something happened to her dog.

As the night wore on, the same kind of compulsion that had sent Ariel off to look for the mare created a struggle within her. She was pulled between her role as Holly's guardian angel and her new assignment. Should she leave the house and go look for the animal? Had the silly dog run off and got himself in trouble by his own foolishness? Or did his disappearance have something to do with possible harm to Shanna and Holly?

Ariel sat on Holly's bed in the midst of Holly's teddy bear, stuffed Peter Rabbit and favorite blanket. The little angel rested her head in her hands. Think, she told herself. She'd done the right thing in keeping Lady safe. The burns on the mare's neck could be important, at least Jay thought so. Maybe Jiggs's disappearance was important, too. There's only one way to find out, she told herself. A brief search wouldn't take her away from the house for very long.

Ariel looked at Holly's sweet, angelic face and made her decision. "I'll find Jiggs," she promised, and laid a feathery kiss on Holly's cheek. "I'll be back in a few minutes."

But earthly minutes were lost in Ariel's concept of time. More than two hours passed before her angelic antenna picked up Jiggs's sharp bark and led her to Lew Walker's run-down cabin on the other side of the hill from Shanna's house.

All kinds of junk littered the property. Jiggs was having a wonderful time racing around chasing cats that must have numbered over a dozen. Felines of every description scurried under the listing cabin and up trees, and peered with rounded yellow eyes out of abandoned stripped cars. Jiggs probably chased one of them home, Ariel reasoned, and found himself in dog heaven.

Amid all the ruckus, the cabin remained dark and silent.

Ariel plopped herself down in front of Jiggs and stopped him in his tracks. ''Fun's over. You're going home.''

He gave a protesting ''woof'' as she grabbed his collar. Floating over him, she firmly directed his short-legged body up the hill behind Shanna's property. They had just reached the crest of the wooded hillside when her celestial awareness of danger exploded with the impact of a meteor.

Chapter Nine

Tongues of orange flames leaped from the spreading liquid as it flowed across old dry floorboards from the back porch into the kitchen. In a matter of seconds, the back of the house was an inferno. Shanna jerked awake and instantly felt the blast of heat and heard the crackling flames. A hideous orange glow lit up the hall.

As she screamed she leaped from her bed without thought or hesitation. Because she'd practiced moving around with limited vision, a dark smoky haze filling the room didn't disorient her. She bounded into the next room where Holly was sleeping and lifted her out of bed.

Holly cried out at the rough treatment and tried to get out of her mother's frantic hold.

"Stop it!" Shanna choked. "Fire." She clutching the child against her breast and blindly crossed the sitting room toward what she hoped was the hall door.

As Ariel flashed into the burning house, she saw in an instant that in a few seconds the fast-moving flames would close off the hall and trap Shanna and Holly in the bedroom—*unless she did something*. What? A force field? She'd never tried one before. Could she do it? There was no time to practice. Summoning all the cosmic energy she could muster and concentrating on one image, she put thought into form. In a split second an impenetrable wall rose between Ariel and the kitchen. As if by a fire line, the encroaching flames were blocked from inching any closer to the bedroom door.

Shanna came staggering out into the hall, pressing Holly's head against her chest and trying to hold back the convulsive coughs racking her chest. The house was already filling up with deadly smoke, and with every breath, she drew more of the deadly fumes into her lungs. At the kitchen door, greedy flames were leaping at some invisible barrier as the back of the house was engulfed in a raging inferno.

Dizzy, blind, Shanna staggered toward the front door. Since her arms were filled with Holly, she couldn't let her hand trail along the wall as Jay had taught her to do. She hit one side of the wall and then the other. Dizzy from the smoke and loss of oxygen, she stumbled and nearly lost her balance. As she reeled blindly around, she couldn't tell where they were in the hall.

Holly's little body began to convulse with racking coughs. She cried against her mother's chest, and her little arms went around Shanna's neck in a stranglehold.

Her child's weight seemed to increase with every step, and rising waves of dizziness threatened to send Shanna to her knees. The smoke-logged air she was pulling into her lungs was having its effect.

Keep moving.

At the same time she heard the inner voice, she suddenly seemed to be floating. Holly felt light in her arms, and her legs moved forward as if propelled by their own volition.

She couldn't see anything. Not the wall. Not the door. Her smarting eyes, streaming with tears, gave back no images. She shifted Holly and, throwing out one of her hands, flayed the air, hoping to touch anything that might be familiar.

When she touched a flat surface directly in front of her, a momentary flicker of relief went through her. A wall! But as she ran her hand over it, the wall gave no clues as to which direction she should go to find the door.

Tears of frustration filled her burning eyes. A new wave of weakness threatened to dissolve the support in Shanna's legs. A slight breeze like a fresh wind touched Shanna's face, and a calming sense of reason reminded her that there was an expanse of wall on both sides of the front door. I must have walked into one of the walls, she thought, but which one?

The one on the right.

A frantic sweep of her hand verified that a doorframe stood just inches from where she and Holly were trapped against the wall. She lurched in that direction, found the doorknob and lock. She sobbed as she turned the key and flung the door open.

"Run," she croaked as she pushed Holly out the door ahead of her. "Run, Holly."

The porch floor rolled under Shanna's stumbling feet as she careened blindly to the porch railing and front steps. Coughing and retching, she made it to the clearing in front of the house before her legs gave way beneath her.

"Mama," Holly cried, and fell into her outstretched arms. The next instant Jiggs bounded into the middle of them, licking their tearful faces and slapping them with his joyful tail.

As black smoke rose to fill the night sky, a mysterious back draft kept the fire from completely consuming Aunt Emma's house.

JAY WAS IN HIS CAR and headed back to Westridge within minutes after he received Skaggs's telephone call.

"They got out in time," the deputy had reassured him. "Took in a little smoke and that's all."

"Did someone check them out?" Jay didn't trust Skaggs's evaluation of their conditions.

"Hell, yes," the officer answered indignantly. "Paramedics from Cedarville looked them over. The mother needed a little oxygen, but that's all. I offered to get an ambo up from Denver, but the lady wasn't having any part of it."

"How'd the fire get started?"

"Don't rightly know," said Skaggs. "We'll have to let the place cool down before we have a look around. Probably faulty wiring or she left something on that caught fire."

"And maybe it was set."

Skaggs swore. "You just won't stop, will you, Doc. I keep telling ya Westridge isn't like that cesspool you call New York. We got respectable folks living here. They don't go setting fires on other people's property."

Jay didn't even listen. Guilt lashed at him. He shouldn't have left her. Every fiber of his being had warned him she was in danger. "Where are they now?"

"At the clinic. Marla's not here, but one of the neighbor women is staying with them."

"I'm on my way."

SHANNA HAD DROPPED OFF into a restless sleep about dawn. About an hour later, she was aware of movement beside her and a medicinal odor brought her to the surface with a jerk. Hospital? Was she back in the hospital?

Like a fast-rewinding tape, her mind reeled backward. She gasped as terror grabbed her again. The fire.

A pair of warm hands closed over hers. "Don't be frightened. I'm here." Jay's reassuring voice broke through her lingering mental haze.

"Where am I?"

"The medics brought you to the clinic. I got here a couple of hours ago. The lady who had been sitting with you went home. And I've been sitting here waiting for you to wake up." He touched her face and eased back a strand of hair that had drifted forward on her cheek.

"Holly?"

"She's asleep in the other bed. And Jiggs is shut up in Marla's apartment."

She closed her eyes against the pain of remembering. No, it couldn't be. This was just another one of her horrible nightmares. But even as she mentally denied the truth, she asked, "The house? Is everything . . . gone?"

"No. From what Skaggs said, the fire was contained in the kitchen area."

"Thank heaven," she breathed.

"He's not sure how it started." Jay knew his jaw was stiff and his mouth tight. He was glad Shanna couldn't read his expression.

Something in his tone made her wonder if he thought she was to blame. Maybe she was. How could she be positive that she hadn't unwittingly done something to cause the fire.

"I made Holly a cup of hot chocolate before bed but I...I thought I had everything turned off." Her lips quivered.

Jay took one of her hands and held it tightly. He wasn't about to frighten her with his gut feeling that the fire had been the "next accident" promised in the call. "When you're rested, you can consider your options."

Options? She swallowed back hysterical laughter. She didn't have any. The means of supporting herself and her child was tied to Aunt Emma's house. The additional cost and inevitable delay would make getting into business even more precarious. "Well, I *did* want to redo the kitchen," she said in a joking tone that hid the desperation she felt.

"The important thing is that both of you got out safely. Nothing else matters. Nothing." A wave of thankfulness brought a tight knot to his chest.

Holly whimpered, and sat up in the next bed. "Mommy?"

"Yes, darling. I'm right here."

"Hi, kiddo." Jay went over to the second bed. "How ya doing?"

"Okay," Holly said feebly.

He carried her over to Shanna's bed, and she cuddled down in her mother's arms. Jay's emotions swirled as he looked down at the tender picture they made. It was a miracle both of them had made it out of the house. "A miracle," he breathed.

His thankful murmur made Shanna remember the unseen force propelling her forward when she had faltered and the inner voice telling her which way to move when she couldn't find the door. She moistened her dry lips and tightened her arm around Holly. "Someone was looking after us."

"Ariel," said Holly in a sleepy voice.

Both adults were quiet, and then Jay said, "Well, thank her for me. I'm certainly glad that pretend friend of yours shows up at the right times."

"She's not pretend." Holly turned her head and looked at the foot of Shanna's bed. "Are you, Ariel?"

Jay followed her gaze, and for the briefest of moments his mind's eye held the impression of a blond little girl perched on the bed railing, looking right back at him with a smile on her angelic face. It couldn't be—but it was.

The same little girl that had stopped his car on the mountain road. Before he could acknowledge such a bizarre impression, his common sense got the better of him and he gave a sheepish laugh. Talk about the power of suggestion.

"Well, tell her thank you from me," Jay repeated as he leaned over and kissed the little girl on the forehead. Then he let his fingers thread the soft ringlets of Holly's hair as she lay with her cheek pressed against her mother's warm face. "You've almost got me convinced, Holly."

"Would you like Ariel to be your friend, too?" she asked solemnly.

"I think she already is."

MARLA RETURNED to the clinic midmorning, just about the time that Shanna and Holly were waking up from their second sleep. The nurse was bewildered to find the place full of people and a dog shut up in her apartment. She put her hand over her mouth in horror when Jay told her what had happened.

She immediately started berating herself for having been away when she was needed. "I should have canceled that dentist appointment. I debated about going, but I knew it would be another month's wait if I didn't. And I'd been putting off shopping for a bunch of stuff I needed . . . but I should have been here."

That makes two of us, thought Jay.

The nurse fussed over Shanna and Holly to the point that both of them felt smothered. Holly put on her belligerent face and refused to leave her mother's side even with bribes of chocolate milk and cinnamon toast.

"The best medicine in the world is a full stomach," Marla proclaimed, and forced a bowl of hot cereal on Shanna. "Now it's time for a warm bath and some clean clothes. I'll run up to the house and get a change of clothing. You're going to feel a lot better when you get the smoke smell out of your hair and skin. I'll be right back."

While she was gone, Jay decided it was time for him to use a little of the nurse's directive attitude. "You and Holly will stay at my dad's place for now. No argument," he said as Shanna opened her mouth. "You'll need time to assess the fire damage, put in an insurance claim and see to repairs. As soon as the house gets livable you can move back in. Until then, the sensible thing to do is accept my father's hospitality."

How diplomatic he was, thought Shanna. He was trying to assure her that she would be his father's guest, not his. But what about the growing need to feel his arms around her? How could she keep from loving him if she was living in the same house with him and the very air she breathed was constantly filled with his essence? Wouldn't it all have a shattering effect on her determination not to presume on his good-hearted compassion? He didn't want to get romantically involved with her. His constant retreat away from any kind of intimacy was evidence enough. Oh, he was attracted to her. He had admitted that. But there was no intention on his part to parlay the growing sexual magnetism into anything that would have a serious impact on his life or career.

"You'll be under no obligation to me—or my father. This is simply the best arrangement at the moment."

Don't think this offer carries any personal commitment on my part, his professional tone seemed to add.

She appreciated him for being so up-front about the offer. As she hesitated, she knew that she had no choice, really, but to accept. With Holly to think about and no funds to find housing elsewhere, his offer was a godsend.

Or an angel-send? thought Ariel smugly.

Chapter Ten

That afternoon, Shanna insisted upon driving by the house before going to Jay's place.

"Are you sure you want to?" Jay asked. He hadn't been by the house himself yet, and he had no idea about the damage. Marla had been out to the house, and when she returned with clothes and Holly's stuffed animals, she told him that only the kitchen and back porch were a disaster area. "Beats me why the whole place didn't go up in smoke. But the fire burned itself out before it reached the hall. I guess the volunteer firemen got there too late to pump water all over everything—blessing in disguise, if you ask me. Except for some smoke damage, the main part of the house remains intact."

Thank heavens for that, breathed Jay, his skin crawling anew with the horror of Shanna and Holly's narrow escape. Even before they reached the house, the air was filled with a lingering pungent odor of burnt wood and smoking ashes.

Shanna braced herself as Jay stopped the car in front of the house. Her heart began to race as he went around and opened the car door. She stepped out. With a dryness like cotton in her mouth, she looked up at the house. She braced herself to see only faint shadows and blurred lines and planes, but a wonderful shock scissored through her. Even though the images were neither sharp nor distinct, she could identify roof lines, glazed panes of windows and even the shadowy relief of the porch railing.

Jay saw the sudden flush of excitement in her face. "What is it?"

"I can almost see."

He gave a relieved and joyful laugh. "Wonderful."

She turned and fixed a steady gaze on his face. His features were still lost in a cloudy perception, but she knew from a wide slash of white teeth that he was smiling broadly. Before long, she'd be able to see him clearly, and her heart tightened at the thought. If his looks halfway matched his voice and touch, he would be more man than any woman had a right to dream about, she warned herself.

Holly and Jiggs bounded from the back seat of the car. "No, Holly! You can't go in," Jay warned as she ran toward the front stairs. Even though Marla had slipped in and out of the house without difficulty, he wasn't sure it was all that safe.

Ariel had already checked out the origin of the fire and was hoping to guide Jay into making his own inspection. Did he also suspect arson? And was there any proof?

"From the front everything looks normal. Let's walk around the house and see what it looks like at the back."

He took her arm, and they made their way through low scrubs and a stand of quaking aspen to the slope of the hill behind the house. As they stood there and surveyed the charred walls and roof, Jay was glad

Shanna couldn't see clearly as they surveyed the damage. The entire back of the house would have to be torn down and rebuilt. Most likely the entire electrical system would have to be replaced. In fact, the old structure had been weakened and damaged to such a point that tearing it down and building a new one would be the really sensible thing to do. The Victorian house was like the mine tailings scarring the mountainside and the old mill falling into the creek. They represented a time past, and even Shanna's dogged stubbornness wasn't going to turn back the clock.

"What do you think?" Shanna asked with forced lightness. "Am I going to get a new kitchen out of the insurance company?"

"At least." He tried to match her optimistic tone. He wondered how much insurance coverage she had on the house, but he wasn't about to pry into her financial matters. She was touchy enough about managing her own affairs, and he certainly wasn't going to point out that she was facing a myriad of costly repairs that were certain to eat up a lot more than what the insurance would pay.

"Wait here," he said. "I'm going to poke around a bit."

Good, thought Ariel. Jay was getting better at picking up telepathic messages. The fire had been set. She knew it, and he needed to know it, too. She was pretty certain that the possibility of arson had already arisen in his mind.

"Are you sure you should?" Shanna asked anxiously.

"Yes," he answered flatly.

With Ariel floating unseen at his side he eased past some burnt timbers and stopped in the doorway of the charred kitchen. Water still lay on the blackened furniture and floor. He frowned as he stood there, asking himself plaguing questions. Had the fire started from natural causes? Or had Shanna left something like a tea towel near a hot burner? The wall behind the stove wasn't as charred as the others.

Look at the floor, ordered Ariel.

At first he didn't notice anything that accounted for a sudden urge to stare down at ashes and charred boards. Then his steady gaze registered a blackened path in the black whorls of charred wood. A burnt track ran from the outside doorway and across the kitchen floor.

As if someone had poured an inflammable material and then lit it.

"Arson," he breathed, and a cold chill attacked his spine. Why would anyone try to burn the house down around Shanna and her child? Every civilized fiber of his being denied that such a person existed. Even though he'd seen horrible human atrocities in his career, the evil against an innocent like Shanna was still beyond comprehension. It had to be a madman. A psychotic lunatic. Someone determined to end her life by any means.

His head jerked around as he heard voices. Shanna was talking with someone. Quickly he made his way through the charred walls, convinced that everyone and everything around her was a potential danger.

He recognized the blond teenage girl. Billie Jo Rendell. She'd been in the clinic once for a refill of birth control pills. The records showed that his father had prescribed them for her nearly a year earlier when she was only fifteen. Jay hadn't pressed her for any personal information, and Billie Jo had been closemouthed about her sexually active life-style. He'd never seen the gangly, narrow-faced youth with her before but guessed that it must be Jasper Dietz, the boyfriend whom Billie Jo's father had called a "bird-brain." Something about the way the two young people fixed stony-eyed glares at the charred house reminded Jay of a couple of hawks eyeing road kill.

Were they wondering what had gone wrong?

Whoever had set the fire certainly hadn't expected it to put itself out with only limited damage to the back of the house. He didn't understand how that had happened himself, but he was thankful for the miracle.

As he walked over to where they were standing, he remembered Shanna's belief that the pair must have made use of the empty house, because Marla had found their schoolbooks in an upstairs bedroom. The newspapers were filled with stories of vindictive young people who would readily trash other people's property just to get even. Was this a case of senseless revenge? He couldn't believe that they'd set fire to Shanna's house just because they'd lost a convenient place to make out. But he didn't understand so many of the things that were going on these days. He'd be damned if any of it made sense.

"Did you see the fire when it started last night?" Jay asked as they continued to stare at the charred walls and smoldering timbers.

"Well, kinda," hedged Jasper. He gave Billie Jo a hesitant look as if he wasn't quite sure how much more to say.

She shrugged her slim shoulders. "We were parked on Devil's Ridge . . . up there." She pointed to a bluff that was west of Shanna's property. "You can see the whole town from that spot."

"We thought it might be her house or one of the cabins when we first noticed the fire," Jasper volunteered.

"You must have been relieved when you found out it wasn't your place?" Shanna said.

With a pursed mouth, Billie Jo answered shortly, "Can't say I'd be sorry if the whole blasted town went up in smoke."

"You don't mean that," Shanna countered sharply. The girl's cold, selfish indifference stunned her. She couldn't imagine anyone even thinking such a thing. "That's a terrible thing to say."

"Billie Jo's a little upset. With her mother dead and everything," Jasper said haltingly. Billie Jo shot him a look that withered his next sentence before it left his mouth. He shifted uncomfortably and stuck his hands in his tight Levi's. His head was slightly lowered as he looked at Jay and Shanna, and even though he was a husky youth, there was something of the hangdog about him, thought Jay. No doubt about who made the calls with that couple. Billie Jo had him on a short leash.

"I was wondering," Jay said casually, "if you had any idea, Billie Jo, how Shanna's photo album ended up in your barn?"

The girl's eyes hardened. "Beats me."

"Someone took it from the house—"

"Well, I didn't."

"And you don't know who did?"

With a fling of her blond head, she snapped, "I suppose it must have been my mother. She was good at lifting stuff she wanted for her column. Wasn't

above slinging a little dirt, if you know what I mean.
I always told her she'd make a great blackmailer.''

Shanna felt sick to her stomach. She couldn't
imagine any daughter talking about her mother that
way.

"Come on, let's get out of here," Billie Jo said to
Jasper, and stomped away with her boyfriend following in her wake like a trained pet.

"Poor girl," Shanna said in a sad tone. "Her
mother's death must have hit her hard. Why else
would she be so vindictive?"

"I don't know," said Jay, thoughtfully. *But I wish
I did.* That pair knew more than they were telling.

On the drive to Deerview, Shanna sat close to Jay,
and they talked quietly about the arrangements he'd
made in Denver for his father and how the elder Dr.
Harrison had insisted that Jay offer his Deerview
home to her. With their heads bent closely together,
they seemed oblivious to anything else around them.

Holly tried to get them to turn around and pay some
attention to her, but they pretty much ignored her attempts. After several tries, a lost look crossed her face
and she was close to tears.

Ariel materialized in the back seat beside her.
"What's the matter, Holly?"

"He likes Mama," she said with a childish whim-
per.

"And he likes you," Ariel said softly. She knew that
Holly felt shut out. "Remember how he played with
you at the park? I bet you'll have lots of fun at his
place. He has a guitar and everything." Ariel smiled,
remembering the warmth of sitting beside him and
singing. If Holly only knew how lucky she was that her

mother had found someone like Dr. Jay to take care of them.

"I want to live in our house," Holly said with childish stubbornness. The fact that the back walls and roof were nothing but a charred mess failed to be of consequence to her.

Ariel sighed. She hoped Holly wasn't going to create problems for her mother and Jay. They had enough to deal with at the moment, and their relationship wasn't yet firm enough to stand any jealous acting-out from Holly.

"What's the matter, honey?" Shanna asked as they got out of the car and she saw her daughter's scowling face. It wasn't like Holly to keep a stony silence. Usually she was chattering a mile a minute about something. "Don't you feel well?"

Holly started crying. "I want to go home."

Shanna knelt down and hugged her. *Home. They didn't have one.* She stroked Holly's soft hair and pressed the little girl's soft, tearful cheek against her own. Shanna choked back a knot in her throat as she murmured reassurances.

Jay's emotions ran the gamut of poignant tenderness to wild anger as he watched them. A feeling of "mine" brought a swell of affection accompanied by pure rage. He knew that he was capable of defending them at any cost to himself. Nothing in the world was as important at that moment than wiping away their tears and putting smiles back on their faces.

"Come on, tiger," Jay said, easing Holly out of Shanna's arms. "You're going to like it here. Let's go say hello to Johnny. I bet he's glad you're going to be around to feed him some more carrots."

"I didn't bring any carrots." Holly glared at Jay as if it was his fault.

"That's all right. We'll find something in the house that he'll like and feed him later." His dad's horse stood alone at the fence, so the Rendell mare must have been picked up and taken to the vet, thought Jay. Good. He was anxious to know what the results of the blood tests were.

Jiggs bounded over to the pasture fence and barked loudly at the horse, but Johnny only swished his tail as if the tiny dog was some kind of an annoying summer fly. In spite of Jay's efforts to get Holly interested in the horse, she wasn't that easily won over, and when he finally set her down, she clung to her mother's side and glowered at Jay as if he might whisk Shanna away from her at any moment.

"Well, shall we go inside and get you two settled?" Jay asked, very much aware of Holly's hostility and the insecurity that she must be feeling. After all that had happened, he wasn't surprised the child was reacting to the trauma. In her childish mind, she might connect all the bad things that had happened with Jay's presence in her mother's life. That might set up a psychological aversion to him that might be hard to break.

As they went through the small house, Jay viewed it from a completely different perspective—would Shanna and Holly be safe here? He wasn't happy to see how easily someone could break into it.

As he walked Shanna around the rooms, she could tell he was trying to put a good face on the situation. He immediately began moving furniture so she would have fewer obstacles as she made her way around the place. He was right about the smaller house posing fewer problems. The kitchen was compact, and she could turn in a circle and practically reach everything. Two bedrooms furnished with twin beds shared a small connecting bathroom. Since Jay was already settled in the front bedroom, Shanna insisted that she and Holly take the back room. As he described the furnishings, she could imagine rooms with no clutter, no frills, and furniture that undoubtedly exemplified masculine practicality.

"We can bring in whatever more you need," Jay offered anxiously. "I know you'll want to get a lot of things out of the house as soon as you can. I could check and—"

"We'll be fine," Shanna told him, painfully aware that he must feel totally trapped in the situation. And why not? Look what had happened! His Good Samaritan rescue had landed him in a net that was drawing him tighter and tighter into more and more obligation for their welfare. She hated being a burden to anyone, especially someone who attracted her on as many different levels as Jay Harrison. Now she was indebted to him for the very roof over their heads. But it was only temporary, she resolved. She wasn't licked yet, not by a long shot. Her chin came up. "We'll be fine here until I can make other arrangements."

"What other arrangements?" he demanded curtly. What in the blazes was going through that stubborn mind of hers?

"Once I find out what the insurance company is going to do and how long it will take to repair the house, I'll be able to make some decisions. I appreciate you and your father's hospitality, but we'll find an interim place of our own as soon as possible."

He clenched his hands so he wouldn't reach out and shake some sense into her. The stubborn woman refused to acknowledge the danger she was in. He was convinced that none of the things that had happened to her were accidents. For one thing, after what he'd seen this morning, he didn't believe the fire was started by electrical wiring or by something she'd left near a hot burner. As far as he was concerned, the same person or persons who had arranged her car "accident" had set fire to her house. Here he was, wanting to build a wall around her for protection, and she was already talking about moving out.

Ariel decided it was a good thing Shanna couldn't see Jay's expression. He looked like a stoked boiler about ready to burst. He opened his mouth and then shut it. He drew in a couple of deep breaths, and then said, "Why don't we just concentrate on getting you and Holly settled in here? You'll need some groceries. I doubt that you and Holly will want to eat canned sardines and pinto beans. Why don't you make a list?"

"I'd rather do my own shopping," she said evenly. "I'm sure we can pick up a few things here at the country store that will tide us over. How about it, Holly? You can be mother's helper and made sure we buy the right things. I'll bet we can find some of those cookies that you like."

Effectively put in my place, thought Jay with begrudging admiration.

By the time they parked in front of the small grocery store, Holly had recovered her good humor and Shanna seemed ready to face the challenges of shopping. Jay had decided that he'd take advantage of having Shanna occupied for a few minutes while he tried to get some questions answered. He wanted to talk to the volunteer fire chief about that dark burned path across the kitchen floor and also wanted to find out if Skaggs had heard anything from the vet.

"While you're shopping, I'm going to stop in and see the deputy." He glanced at his watch. "Why don't you wait for me in the café next door if you get through before I do? We'll have a bit of supper before we go back to Deerview."

"Sounds good," she agreed, happy to escape the trials of trying to fix supper in a strange kitchen or of feeling totally useless while Jay set food on the table. She nodded as he guided her into the store. For a brief moment panic set in as everything looked like shadowy specters in a dark forest. She realized then that she'd been overly optimistic thinking she could handle the shopping chore by herself. She'd never be able to find everything she needed.

"Hi, Davey. How ya doing today?" Jay greeted someone moving toward them.

"Fine, Dr. Jay. My knee's almost as good as new. I told the coach I'll be ready for next ski season, for sure."

"Davey, this is Mrs. Ryan and Holly. I bet they could use a young fellow like you to show them around."

"Sure, thing, Doc. My dad says I know the place better than he does." He gave a youthful laugh. "'Course, I put everything away, so it's no wonder nobody else can find it."

"You got Little Debbie cookies?" Holly asked.

"Sure thing. Come this way."

Jay gave Shanna's arm a reassuring squeeze. "See you later."

Grateful for his sensitivity, she murmured, "Thanks." Impulsively she reached up and touched his face, and when she felt his cheek muscles move, she knew he was smiling at her.

ARIEL FLOATED ALONG beside Jay as he crossed the street and entered Skaggs's office. A slight, sharp-eyed man wearing a sheriff's badge was sitting behind the deputy's desk. Thank heavens, breathed Jay. Now maybe he could have an intelligent conversation about the things happening to Shanna.

"Sheriff Dunbar?" Jay held out his hand. "I'm Dr. Harrison. I spoke to Deputy Withers in Cedarville yesterday."

The sheriff gave a short nod of his head. "I'm glad you dropped in, Doctor. Saved me the trouble of hunting you up." He leaned forward and his bright eyes centered on Jay as if not even a flicker of an eyelash was going to escape him. "Now, tell me what this is all about."

Good, thought Ariel. It was about time somebody started listening. She nodded in approval as Jay expressed his growing suspicions that Shanna's car had been tampered with and that the fire in her home had been set.

"Those are pretty strong assumptions. I suppose you have some evidence to support them?"

Tell him about the fire pattern, Ariel coached, and watched the sheriff's face as Jay described the dark path of fire across the floor. "As if something had been poured and then lighted."

"I had somebody check the place today, and he didn't find anything suspicious. No canisters of inflammable materials. But there was a burnt cloth near the stove area. I understand that Mrs. Ryan is nearly blind—"

"I don't believe that she is responsible for the fire."

"You're entitled to your opinion, of course. I understand that you and the lady have become quite . . . good friends."

"Yes, we have." Jay met the man's eyes squarely. Dammit, he wasn't going to defend his feelings for Shanna. It was nobody's blasted business. Small towns! Hadn't the twentieth century reached this place yet?

Sheriff Dunbar looked slightly amused, as if he enjoyed ruffling feathers now and then. "Is there something else bothering you, Dr. Harrison?"

"Shanna received a threatening telephone call—I hope Skaggs told you about it."

"He did. He believes that somebody decided to use Mrs. Ryan's car accident to frighten her out of Westridge. Apparently newcomers aren't welcomed by everyone in this close-knit little town, and circumstances are just playing into someone's prejudice. Unless we have some evidence to the contrary—"

"What about Janet Rendell's death? Is that just a happenstance, too? Have you gotten the results of the mare's blood test?"

His eyes narrowed. "I know what you were expecting, Doctor, but I hate to disappoint you. The horse's blood tested normal. There was nothing in her bloodstream to explain the animal's attack on her owner."

"What about the burns on the neck?"

"We're looking into that. Skaggs is over at the Rendells' now. Maybe there's a simple explanation."

"And maybe there isn't."

The officer leaned back in Skaggs's big chair. "Mrs. Ryan's photo album showing up at the scene of the tragedy is a bit of a puzzler. She seems to be tied into a lot of unpleasantness, doesn't she?"

"Someone took the album. An intruder."

"Oh, did she catch someone in the house?"

"No, but the dog raised an alarm. And she found the front door unlocked when she was sure she had locked it earlier."

Sheriff Dunbar looked skeptical. "This lady's arrival in Westridge seems to have made a nice sleepy town into a bed of unpleasant happenings. The question facing us, Dr. Harrison, is why."

There was a weighted silence, and Ariel was hoping that the two men would come up with a different list of motives, but she was disappointed when Jay finally said, "Maybe someone wants her property, but I'll be damned if I know why. I'm sure there are better houses all over the area that are for sale."

"Tell me about her background. We can run a check, of course."

"She's a widow. Has one child, a girl, five years old. Her husband was in the army and was killed in a helicopter accident about a year ago. Apparently he left Shanna very little in the way of insurance or army pension, and when she inherited her aunt's property she came here with the intention of turning the house into a B and B. There's nothing devious or deceptive about her."

"How long have you know her, Dr. Harrison?"

"Since the accident. Not long, I admit but—"

I know her! Ariel unwittingly sent a rush of air across the desk, fluttering papers. She'd been Holly's Guardian Angel since the little girl was a baby. Nothing that Shanna had done was to blame for what was happening to her. Nothing!

Jay reacted with the same kind of denial. "Shanna Ryan is honest, forthright, a loving mother and a very courageous lady. She deserves to be protected from some psycho trying to do her harm."

"Let me get this straight, Dr. Harrison. You think someone sabotaged Shanna Ryan's car and set fire to her house. And you want me to believe that someone entered her house, stole the album and planted it in the Rendells' barn just to make trouble for her?"

Yes. Yes. Ariel couldn't see why there was any question about it. She concentrated on sending the sheriff a red-tagged order. *Don't waste time arguing. Follow up on what Jay is telling you.* But the sheriff wasn't open to Ariel's extrasensory input.

"I'm sorry, but I'm inclined to agree with Deputy Skaggs," Dunbar said. "Three unfortunate accidents don't add up to anything but three unfortunate accidents. Unless something happens to change my mind—"

"Like a successful attempt on Shanna's life?" Jay stood up. "Thank you for your time, Sheriff." He growled, "If Mrs. Ryan turns up dead, I'll be sure and let you know."

Chapter Eleven

Jay loaded Shanna's groceries into the Bronco and then guided her and Holly into a small restaurant that had no air-conditioning and an open cooking grill, making the poorly ventilated room hot and muggy. The smell of fried potatoes mingled with odors of steak and hamburger grease, and the smoky air was thick enough to cut. An aging cook wearing a dirty apron lined up orders on a counter with all the finesse of someone filling a horse trough.

A gum-popping waitress shook her flaming red hair when Jay asked for a booth. The only empty table was near the front windows, and every head in the room seemed to turn in their direction as they sat down.

The waitress spouted the day's specials as "crispy fried chicken" and "spaghetti and meatballs." Shanna and Jay ordered the chicken, and true to her culinary tastes, Holly chose the spaghetti.

Shanna sat across the table from Jay with Holly on her right, and she was conscious of his long legs moving close to hers as he shifted in his chair. She didn't need to see his face to know that he was deep in thought and had his mind on something more than a questionable meal of crispy fried chicken. If Holly hadn't been there, she would have demanded to know why he was wound up tighter than a spring.

He had been unusually withdrawn and uncommunicative when he loaded the groceries into the car, and Shanna guessed that his visit to Skaggs's office had not gone well.

They had been waiting for their orders a few minutes when he suddenly jerked to life. Waving, he called out, "Hi, there. Won't you join us, Ted?"

Shanna smelled the liquor on the man's breath even before he reached their table. Why on earth had Jay invited him to join them?

The only empty chair was on her left, and Jay saw him give Shanna a glazed look as he plopped down with a slurred, "Sorry."

Just exactly what the "sorry" referred to wasn't at all clear to Shanna. Was the man apologizing for his intrusion, his intoxicated state, or was it an expression of sympathy because of the fire? She couldn't see his face, but it didn't take much insight to know that the man was drunk.

Jay poured a cup of coffee out of the pot the waitress had left on the table and handed it to Ted. "Here, have some black coffee."

The Texan wrapped his big-knuckled fingers around the cup to steady it, but spilled some of the liquid getting it to his mouth. After a couple of sips, he set the cup down so abruptly that some coffee spilled over the side. "Real sorry," he mumbled. "Bad thing, fire."

What thoughts were chasing around in the man's inebriated mind? Jay decided to try to find out. "There's plenty of brush between your property and Shanna's, isn't there, Ted? I bet you're thanking your lucky stars the blaze didn't race down the hill to your place. It could have easily enough.''

"Hell, that's all I need about now."

Jay felt a little guilty for taunting him, but he needed some answer that maybe Ted could give him. "I guess you're glad it was your neighbor's bad luck and not yours. A fire could wipe you out, couldn't it?"

"Your place wasn't in any danger, Ted," Shanna said, trying to make up for Jay's insensitivity. "And only the back of mine burned."

Ted rested his arms on the table, his head lowered as if too heavy for his neck. "How'd the damn thing get started?"

"Nobody seems to be sure," Jay answered. "I was wondering if you had any ideas."

Ted stiffened as he lifted his head up and glared at Jay with bloodshot eyes. "What in the hell you getting at?"

"Oh, you know how rumors get started," Jay bluffed. "Some folks are thinking that you might be able to get your hands on that property cheap if there wasn't a house sitting on it."

Instead of the bombastic retort that Jay expected, Ted just slumped back in the chair. All starch drained from his lean body, and his mouth went slack. "I wouldn't give a damn if the whole town burned down."

Shanna was startled. *His daughter had said much the same thing.*

Jay opened his mouth to prod him further, but the waitress arrived at that moment with their orders and effectively put an end to any conversation while she unceremoniously deposited their plates around the table. When she asked if Ted wanted to order, he just shook his head. "Just coffee."

Shanna gave her attention to Holly, making sure she had a napkin around her neck to catch the spaghetti that was bound to fall off her fork. As far as her own meal was concerned, she decided "fingers first" was the way to go with her two pieces of fried chicken.

Jay seemed more interested in talking than eating. He made a few idle comments about Westridge and the fondness his father had for the place. "I guess property value here is bound to increase just like it has every place else. I heard somewhere, Ted, that you were thinking about building a lodge."

"That was Jan's idea, not mine. She was always talking about what could be done with that old Victorian house. She had a bunch of cockamamy ideas about turning it into some kind of lodge. When the old lady died, she was sure it would go up for sale. If you want to know the truth, I was kinda glad when Mrs. Ryan decided to keep the place."

"Do you know anybody who might want to force Shanna to sell that property by burning down her house?"

Ted's mouth gave an ugly twist as his belligerent mood returned. "No, I don't. And you'll have a hell of a time pinning it on me."

Shanna quickly put her hand on his arm. "The fire just happened. No one's to blame."

Jay restrained himself. How much longer could he keep from telling Shanna his growing suspicion that the fire was deliberately set. If only he had some concrete proof of arson.

"I'll be needing a good neighbor like you," Shanna told Ted.

"You're not moving out, then?"

"No. My plans are the same. This will be a set-back, but I'm still determined to rebuild and get into business as a B and B as soon as I can." She was pleased that her voice was firm and businesslike.

Ted sighed. "Well, I may put my place on the market. Living here without Jan isn't going to be the same. She was the one who wanted to leave Texas. Billie Jo didn't want to move to Colorado, and once we got here, she went haywire. Hell, I don't even know my daughter anymore. Thumbing her nose at me. Shacking up with that deadbeat Jasper." He rubbed a hand across his eyes. "I never could handle Billie Jo the way Jan could. The two of them fought like two stray cats, but her mother always kept the upper hand—until Jasper showed up. And now that she's gone . . ."

Shanna couldn't see his eyes, but she was sure there were tears in them. Jay felt a little guilty as he prodded a raw wound, but he had Shanna and Holly to think about. "I heard Deputy Skaggs was at your place today, looking around."

Ted nodded. "Yeah. He spent a lot of time poking his nose into everything. Asking a bunch of fool questions. They found the mare, you know. Showed up in somebody's pasture. They told me that some vet took her into Cedarville for some tests. Don't know why in the hell they're wasting time putting her down. She's a killer. I'd have finished her off quick enough if I'd found her."

Jay didn't tell him that they'd found the mare in his father's pasture. He still hadn't figured that one out. "Did Skaggs say what he was looking for at your place?"

"Naw, but he went over the barn pretty good. Asked a lot of questions about the workbench I've got out there. Don't know why he was so blasted interested in all my tools. You can't believe what the SOB took for himself?"

"What?" Jay's chest was suddenly tight.

"A soldering gun.

"A soldering gun?" Jay echoed. *With a hot, round point!* Jay struggled to keep the excitement out of his voice. "You had a soldering gun in the barn?"

"I keep all kinds of tools out there on my workbench. Comes in handy when I'm doing repairs and other stuff. That blasted deputy poked around like he was making a Christmas list. When I told him to keep his sticky hands off my stuff, he just laughed. Doing his duty, he said. Can you beat that? He carries off my soldering gun, and I can't do a damn thing about it."

"Did he take anything else?"

"Who in the hell knows? I wasn't watching him every minute. He could have ripped off a bunch of my stuff right under my nose. I'll probably never see any of it again."

Shanna had heard the excitement in Jay's voice. "What do think it means?" she asked, directing her gaze in his direction. Once again she was frustrated by not being able to read his expression. She'd never realized how much eyes revealed what a person was thinking.

"I don't know," he admitted honestly. He certainly wasn't going to speculate with Ted taking in every word. Deciding to change the subject, he asked casually, "By the way, did Skaggs ask you about Shanna's photo album?"

"Yeah, I told him I'd never seen the damn thing." He turned to Shanna. "When Jan was writing about someone, she liked to get in some personal stuff. Maybe more than she should have. You know what I mean? Just out of high school, she worked once as an assistant to Laura Laureau, who became one of them Hollywood columnists. I guess it got in her blood. Lots of time she got angry calls about something that she'd printed. If she asked for your album—"

"She didn't. And I hadn't even unpacked it yet when your wife came to see me. I'm sure it was still upstairs in one of the moving boxes. I didn't even know it was gone until Skaggs brought it back."

"Then, blast it all, how'd it get to my place? You're saying someone carried the damn book out of the house without your knowing it and stuck it behind a bale of hay in my barn? That's too crazy. If you didn't give it to Jan, then—?"

"How'd did it get in your barn?" finished Jay.

He put a hand up to his forehead as if trying to ward off sudden pain. Then he took a deep breath and straightened up. "I don't know if Jan hid it there, but I guess it's no use pretending it couldn't have been her. Jan thought of herself as a journalist and...and I suppose she'd do almost anything to get a good story. She was a smart gal, Jan was. A pain sometimes. But life is going to be a crock without her."

The anguish in his voice made Shanna feet guilty. They shouldn't be talking about his dead wife in such a callous way. She touched his arm. "I'm sorry, Ted, truly sorry. If there's any way I can help."

"Sounds like you've got enough on your plate already. But thanks." He got up. "I think I'll head on home. Maybe Billie Jo will be there."

Jay watched him lumber unsteadily out the door. "Well, my respect for Deputy Skaggs has gone up a little. At least he's checking out some possibilities. If the burns on Lady's neck match...?" He cut short his speculation. He didn't want to elaborate in Holly's presence. Even though the little girl didn't seem to be much interested in the adult conversation, he would bet she was taking in every word.

Shanna pushed back her plate, suddenly feeling sick to her stomach. "You don't think... the soldering gun... the horse...?"

"I don't know what to think," he said aloud, but silently thought, *I bet the wounds on the mare's neck match the soldering gun.*

"I feel sorry for Ted," said Shanna. "Someone ought to shake that daughter of his. He's really hurting, and I haven't seen a sign that Billie Jo cares a damn."

"I wonder what her real relationship with her mother was. If Jan was putting pressure on Billie Jo to break off with Jasper..."

"Surely, you don't think that the girl had anything to do with her mother's... accident."

Ariel didn't wait to hear Jay's reply. Her attention was drawn to a familiar figure going down the sidewalk in front of the café. She flashed outside and followed Lew Walker. The man must be heading for his old pickup truck parked a few feet down the street. Ever since Ariel had found Jiggs at Lew's place, she'd been wanting to get Jay up there to look around.

Now would be a good time.

As Ariel came up behind the wizened little man and floated along after him, she wasn't exactly sure what she intended to do. When she saw that Lew had his keys dangling in one hand, she decided.

"Hello there," she said, materializing beside him.

He turned his head, and at the same instant she stuck out her little foot and tripped him. As he threw out his hands trying to catch himself, he dropped his keys. Even before it hit the ground, the key ring went sailing off into the dark recesses of a nearby alley. He'd be lucky to find them before next winter, she thought with satisfaction.

Now I have to get Jay out of the cafe.

Lew sprawled on the sidewalk, shaking his fist at the blond-headed girl who raced back to the café and stuck her face against the front window.

Ariel waved frantically to get Jay's attention. He didn't see her but Holly did. "Ariel! There's Ariel." Holly laughed and pointed at the window.

Jay looked up. He couldn't believe his eyes. It was her! The little girl who had flagged him down on the highway. He jumped up. "Be back in a minute."

He hurried out the front door, but as he looked up and down the street, no little girl. Where had she gone? He saw Lew Walker sprawled on the sidewalk, and when Jay realized the man must have fallen, he hurried over to him. "Are you all right? What happened?"

"Some damn kid tripped me. If I get my hands on her—"

"Her? What'd she looked like? How big was she?"

Lew squinted at him. "You know the brat?"

"I'm not sure. Was she small, blond and about ten years old?"

He nodded. "That sounds about right. After she tripped me, she ran back to the café and peered in the window."

"Did you see where she went after that?"

"Funny thing." He scratched his head. "She was there one minute and gone the next. You know what I mean?"

Jay nodded. He had rushed out of the café so fast that the little girl couldn't have had time to take more than a few steps away from the window. He didn't have the foggiest idea of what was going on. Holly seemed to be the only one who understood this girl she called Ariel.

Lew began walking around where he had fallen, searching the sidewalk.

"What are you looking for?"

"My keys. I dropped them when I fell. Couldn't have gone very far."

Ariel smiled smugly as she sat on the hood of Lew's pickup and watched the two men hunt for a set of keys. *Cold, cold, cold.* She giggled. Hiding something from Holly and playing the "hot and cold" game was a favorite of theirs. Too bad the men didn't seem to be enjoying the game.

"Do you have a second set?" asked Jay finally when their search didn't turn up any keys.

"Yep. Always have an extra key or two. I ain't hankering to walk three miles to get them, though." He eyed Jay. "If I was to get a ride up to my place—"

Jay smiled. "Why don't I give you a lift? You'll have to wait a minute, though."

"Sure thing." said Lew, leaning up against his truck. He fished for a cigarette. "I ain't in no hurry."

Jay went back in the café and Ariel gave herself a pat on the back for a job well done when they all piled into the Bronco and Jay drove the winding road to Lew's place.

"Look, kitties," Holly squealed as Jay braked in front of the cabin. Cats of all sizes bounded away from their car. The sight was an eerie one, but Holly was delighted. "Can I hold one?"

"Fine by me," said Lew. "There's a new litter in that old Chevy over there. You can take your pick."

"No," said Shanna firmly. "No kitten. Jiggs is enough of a handful. You can pet one, but we're not taking one home." *Home.* There was that word again. She'd never identified with the homeless before, but now she realized how that one word could bring joy or anguish.

"Just be a minute. I think I know right where the spare keys are," Lew said just before disappearing into the small cabin.

"Come on, kiddo, let's take a look at the kittens," Jay said to Holly, helping her out of the car.

"Jay. No kitten," warned Shanna.

"Relax. We won't slip one in our pockets." Holly's eyes brightened as if that might be a possibility. "I just want to take a look around." He wasn't interested in kittens or cats, but the abandoned cars in various stages of repair interested him very much.

As Jay wandered into a small, open shed filled with tools and spare parts, Ariel entertained a glow of satisfaction. This is what she had wanted Jay to see.

He let out a slow whistle. *Lew Walker knew cars.* Most of the tools and equipment looked old and secondhand, and the light was too dim for any kind of an adequate inventory, but everything that someone working on old cars would need was crammed into that small building. Lew could have sabotaged Shanna's car with ease.

"I want to see the kitties," Holly said, pulling on Jay's hand. He only half listened to Holly's squeals when they viewed four white balls of fur nesting on the floor of a doorless old Chevy. The mother cat was nowhere to be seen, and the kittens were all mewing loudly. "Poor babies," murmured Holly as she petted all of them and, one by one, held their softness against her cheek.

When Lew came up behind them, Jay stiffened. In the few minutes the man had been in the house, Jay's whole perception of him had changed. He wanted to grab him by his scrawny throat and demand to know if he was the one who was threatening Shanna's life. Common sense warned him to go slowly. Alerting the man before any evidence was found would only put him on guard.

"I'm thinkin' one of these might be the right one," Lew said as he dangled a tarnished ring with several keys on it. Can't be sure, though. Till I check 'em out."

"I suppose you could break into your truck if you had to. Looks like you know your way around cars. You've got yourself quite a few old junkers. What do you do with them?"

"Try to get them running. Some of them I tear down for parts. Folks around here say I'm a better mechanic than the guy who owns the gas station. If I had a little money I'd get my own business. Wouldn't take much."

"I guess you're disappointed that Shanna's aunt didn't leave you a little something."

Even in the dim light, Jay could see his eyes narrow. "Emma never had much. Just the house, and I ain't kin. Don't be thinking I was expecting anything."

Jay didn't believe him for one second. If Lew had been as close to Emma as he claimed, he must have hoped that she'd send a little money his way when she died. He could have given into his resentment by fixing Shanna's car, and he might have decided to burn the house down if he couldn't have it. Jay made a mental note to put all this in front of Skaggs and demand that he check out Lew's place as completely as he had the Rendells'.

As expected, Holly put up a fuss for a kitten, but Shanna was firm. They drove back to Main Street with little conversation. Jay let Lew off at his pickup without offering to wait to see if he had the right key. Holly was tired and fussing about the kitty she couldn't have.

When Jay pulled up in front of his father's house, Shanna didn't say anything, but he saw the worried look on her face deepen. She must be feeling about as displaced as a refugee, he thought. He wished that the choice had been theirs and not circumstance that had brought them together to share the physical intimacy of his father's house.

He wanted to share all of this with her, tell her how glad he was that she was here with him, but he was afraid she would misunderstand and think it was just a line. He needed to tread lightly, since being here with him was not of her own choosing.

"Well, here we are. The old homestead," he said lightly. "Time to hunker down for the night."

Jiggs's enthusiastic greeting when Jay opened the door was better than a welcome mat. The mutt greeted each one with sloppy, wet kisses and bounded around in circles at their feet. Holly giggled, Shanna laughed and Jay's eyes twinkled at the dog's antics. The small house filled with sounds of a happy home, and in that shared moment, they became a family joined together in the expressive love of a dog.

Groceries were quickly put away, Holly bathed and put to bed, and when the house was still, Jay slipped his arm around Shanna's waist. "How about some air?"

Being with her and Holly had touched some latent springs of happiness he'd never known existed. His perspective of what was important in life was shifting.

They went out on the porch and sat down in an old swing that creaked as Jay pushed it lightly with his foot. Shanna leaned back in the circle of his arm, listening to a serenade of crickets and the flowing waters of the creek behind the house.

Jay gave a soft laugh. "The lack of city noise drove me nuts at first. I couldn't sleep because it was too damn quiet. No beeper beeping, no telephone ringing—I felt completely cut off. I missed the frantic, hectic pace of city. Couldn't wait to get back." He sighed, "Strange, sitting here with you, surrounded by silent high cliffs and whispering pine trees, it's hard to believe that a short three-hour flight will take me back into the world I left."

Shanna tried to ignore the tightening in her chest. She'd known from the beginning that he'd be returning to New York any day. "It'll seem like you've never been away after a few days."

"That's all it will take?" He turned her head so that he could look down into her face. "A few days? I don't think so. I just wish—I wish we'd met under different circumstances. If you weren't struggling with a handicap and faced with so many stressful problems, you might know your own mind and—"

"What?" She stiffened. "Are you saying I don't know my own mind?"

"I'm saying you're terribly vulnerable right now. You can't trust your feelings—"

"*I* can't trust them—or *you* can't trust them?" she challenged.

He didn't know quite how she had put him on the defensive. He was just trying to explain why he couldn't respond the way he wanted to to the physical attraction that had flared between them.

"Because my eyesight isn't twenty-twenty, I couldn't possibly know that I love you totally and completely?"

She had the satisfaction of hearing his sharp intake of breath before he asked, "Are you sure? I mean, really sure?"

"Well, if I knew my own mind, I would say yes, definitely. But since—"

He didn't let her finish. His mouth captured hers in a kiss that eliminated the need for any more words. The time for talking and protesting was past. He knew that by some miracle, he'd found the woman who would change his life forever.

As he lifted his lips from hers and gently touched her cheek, he felt awed by the delicate beauty of her face. In the gentle wash of moonlight, her hair glistened like spun gold laced with copper. He marveled that beneath her captivating feminine loveliness lay a valiant and courageous spirit as strong as tensile steel. Her bravery, her willpower and her refusal to give up filled him with a love that went far beyond the physical attraction she had always held for him. She had invaded every level of his being. And she loved him. The wonder of it made his voice husky as he stood up and held out his hand. "Let's go inside."

When their clothes lay in a tumbled heap beside his bed, he gathered her to him. All his senses vibrated with the sweet nakedness of her breasts, thighs and legs pressed against his. As he kissed and caressed her, a radiating warmth invaded the deepest level of his consciousness and touched his spirit with a renewing joy. "I found you," he said in wonder and murmured words of love that flowed from the deepest recesses of his heart.

Chapter Twelve

When Shanna awoke the next morning she was alone in Jay's twin bed. As she remembered how they had slept with their bodies cupped together like spoons, a smile curved her lips. She had fallen asleep with his arm over her and his legs intertwined with hers. She couldn't believe that such a wondrous thing had happened to her. Never had she experienced such heights of fulfillment nor an explosion of such joy as when he'd made love to her. For the first time, she'd been a participant in the giving and taking that had brought woman and man together. The inadequacy of her vision only heightened her sensual pleasure in touch. She wanted to touch him, feel every inch of his vibrant body, and know him as part of herself. Her boldness almost shocked her.

He had groaned as her stroking fingertips slid over his tingling skin, exploring every line and curve in his body. She stroked him with the tenderness of a sculptress shaping the male body to fit hers.

This is what real love is, she'd thought with the bewilderment of someone who had never really known it before. For the first time, her mind and spirit were totally engaged in loving and being loved. And when they came together, the union was a happening that was totally new and compelling.

She had slept deeply, and a languid contentment still enfolded her as she listened to Jay moving around in the kitchen. No sign that Holly was up and about yet. She sighed, closed her eyes and let herself float away into that refreshing state between sleeping and dreaming.

Jay had just made coffee and was buttering a piece of toast when the sharp ring of the telephone broke the house's hushed morning stillness. He tried to grab the receiver before the phone's intruding sound awakened Shanna and Holly.

"Dr. Jay, it's Marla. I hate to bother you, but I just got a call. There's been an accident. The McIntyre boy got his arm caught in a combine. Don't know how bad it is. His mother called the clinic and I relayed the message to 9-1-1 for the paramedics."

"Where do they live?"

"About twenty miles west of town. I decided to call you because you could beat the ambo by at least thirty minutes."

Jay grabbed a pencil. "Give me directions." He made a scribbled note, hoping that it'd make sense when he got on the road. "Okay. I'll be on my way."

"I'll call and tell the family you're coming."

"Yes, and Marla..." Jay hesitated. He knew that Shanna would resent his asking the nurse to keep her company while he was gone, but a nagging uneasiness made him want someone with her. "Could you pop over to my place and have a cup of coffee with Shanna while I'm gone?"

"Sure thing. I've got some muffins in the oven. If your dad still has some of those strawberry preserves I put up, we'll have ourselves a treat."

Jay chuckled. "I have a suspicion you know his larder better than we do."

She gave a breezy laugh. "I reckon I do."

He hung up and turned around just as Shanna appeared in the doorway. Her hair was mussed and her face soft with rosy tints of sleep. The sight of her and the memory of last night once again filled him with a sense of wonder. This passionate, courageous, utterly desirable woman had brought new meaning into his life. Now he knew what it meant to fall in love; utterly and completely. His heartbeat quickened just looking at her.

"Who was that?"

"Marla. Worse luck. Some kid got his arm caught in a combine. It's important to that family that I get there and help as soon as possible. Not the way I wanted the day to start." He pulled her into his arms, and his lips sought hers for a hurried kiss. "I guess you know, a doctor's life is never his own. I can't imagine that I'd be happy doing anything else, but at times like this I wish I had a nine-to-five job. I'll be back as soon as I can, love," he promised.

"What about your breakfast?" she asked with wifely concern.

"I'll get something later. Coffee's made. Bread's in the toaster. There's cold cereal in the cupboard by the window. Marla will be over shortly with some hot muffins. Ask her what you need to know about the place. I'm betting she and my dad have been playing house."

A safe bet, thought Shanna. When she'd been putting away some of her things, she'd found a woman's silk robe hanging in the closet.

"I should be back in a couple of hours," Jay said as he picked up his medical bag and headed for the door.

"Take care," she called after him.

"Always. And sweetheart ..." He paused in the doorway.

"Yes?"

He said huskily, "I love you."

A simple declaration filled with a promise for a lifetime. His features were more distinct than she'd ever seen before. Her vision was clearing, slowly but surely. His silhouette against the bright sunshine brought a tightness to her chest and a fullness to her eyes. Last night's ecstasy rushed back. She searched for words to reveal the depths of her feelings for him, but all her full heart could manage was, "I love you, too."

After he'd gone, Shanna made her way around the kitchen, humming softly under her breath, smiling for no reason at all. Every now and then she stopped, hugged herself and sang softly, "I'm in love...in love with a wonderful guy!"

Marla arrived about thirty minutes later, bringing the promised hot muffins. By that time Holly had been fed and was sitting on the front step with Jiggs.

"Good morning," Marla said merrily, and offered the little girl a freshly baked muffin.

Holly took it and held out her other hand for a second. "Jiggs wants one."

"Dogs don't like muffins."

"Jiggs does," Holly insisted.

"Well, they're not good for him," Marla countered in her no-nonsense way. The nurse went into the house, leaving Holly glaring after her with a pugnacious pursing of her lips.

"Give Jiggs some of yours," Ariel admonished as she materialized and sat down on the front step beside Holly. From her closed expression, Ariel knew that the little girl had shut her out. Holly didn't even see her sitting there. That was the way with mortals. They could close the door whenever they wished.

Ariel faded from view as Holly got to her feet and stomped around the side of the house. Jiggs bounded along at her heels, poking his nose as close as he could to the muffin clutched in her hand.

Shanna had told Holly to stay close, but Ariel knew that the child was going to disobey her mother when her determined little steps took her around to the back of the house and along a wooded path near the creek.

"Time to go back, Holly," Ariel said, materializing beside her once again.

No response. The little girl didn't even slow her steps and seemed totally unaware of the angel's presence. Holly had closed off her pretend playmate. Without a willingness to believe, the child no longer saw or heard her. All psychic awareness was gone. Ariel knew she'd lost contact with the little girl, and this was the worst possible time for Holly to shut her out.

The rushing, white-foamed creek presented immediate danger. The current was much too fast for a child like Holly to keep her footing if she slipped off the bank. She'd be battered by rapid waters spewing over jagged rocks and forming swirling eddies in deep green pools.

Ariel hovered close as the child and dog wandered farther and farther downstream. Her repeated admonitions, *"Go back, Holly,"* went unnoticed.

The little girl made a game of throwing sticks in the water and then racing along to follow them as fast as she could. Jiggs bounded along at her side. When they reached a collection of fallen logs spanning one side of the stream to another, the dog lightly ran across the biggest log and then stood on the other side, wagging his tail.

SHANNA ENJOYED A SECOND cup of coffee and two of Marla's hot muffins as they talked about Deerview and the clinic. Marla told Shanna she'd been working with Dr. Harrison, senior, for four years. They both loved Westridge—fishing, jeeping and cross-country skiing. "God's country for sure," she told Shanna. "I've been waiting all my life to find this kind of peace and happiness."

Me, too, Shanna echoed silently. She wondered if Marla could see the secret happiness she felt. No doubt her heightened color and bemused expression confirmed exactly what Marla suspected.

"I like Dr. Jay well enough," Marla said as if following Shanna's thoughts. "But his father has a certain kind of charisma. I don't know how to explain it."

"I hope you won't mind my asking, but are you and the doctor...more than just professional colleagues?"

Marla was silent, and Shanna didn't know if she was angered by the personal question or just weighing her answer. Shanna wished she could see her face clearly. "I'm sorry, I didn't have any right to ask that."

"I suppose you know I've spent time with him here?"

"Yes, I found a woman's robe in the closet. I thought it might be yours."

"Well, then, I guess there's no use pretending. This last year, our relationship changed. We'd been good friends all along, but the more time we spent together, the closer we became. Bradley and I enjoyed doing outdoor things together—and then he had his bypass surgery. I thought I was going to lose the first chance of happiness I ever had. But he's going to be all right."

"I'm happy for you, Marla," Shanna said sincerely.

"I never thought I'd find somebody like Bradley who'd be interested in me. I'm no beauty by a long shot. And at first I couldn't believe it could happen to me. All the men in my life have been mostly scum."

"Jay thinks a lot of his father—"

"And you," Marla added bluntly. "I could see that coming. The first time Dr. Jay mentioned your name, the truth was all over him. So, I've been honest with you. What's in the future for you two?"

"I honestly don't know. We haven't had time to sort things out yet." *But he loves me.*

"He's been pretty concerned about you. Kinda pulled in two directions, it seems to me."

"What do you mean?"

"You know, wanting to get back to New York and yet not wanting to leave his dad. And now he has you to think about, too. Something's got to give."

Her words sobered Shanna, and her pride kicked in again. "I'm not ready to make any decisions until my vision gets back to normal and I find out exactly where

I stand financially. It wouldn't be fair to Jay to do anything impulsively. And there's Holly to think about—'' She broke off, listening. "I better check on her. She's used to playing on the hill behind my aunt's house."

"Stay put. I'll check on her," Marla said quickly. "She was sitting on the porch with the dog when I came in. I think she's a little peeved at me because I wouldn't give her a second muffin."

"I bet she wanted one for Ariel," Shanna said knowingly.

"Ariel?"

"Her little imaginary friend. Holly manages to get double treats that way. One for her, and one for Ariel, only, of course, she ends up eating both things."

"Smart little girl," Marla said with a chuckle. "Only this time she told me it was Jiggs who wanted the second one. She's a pistol, all right. You're going to have your hands full with her. How does she get along with Dr. Jay?"

"Most of the time very well. But lately...well, I have the feeling that she's kind of jealous of him. Doesn't want to share her mommy with anyone else."

"Natural enough. But I bet he'll win her over." Marla left the kitchen, and Shanna heard her footsteps echoing across the porch and down the steps. "Holly? Holly? Where are you?"

Shanna waited a moment, and when Holly didn't answer, she pushed back her chair and cautiously made her way to the front door.

"I don't see her," Marla said as Shanna came out on the front porch. "I went all the way around the house."

"Is she over by the pasture watching Johnny?"

"Don't see her by the fence. The horse is grazing in the far corner of the pasture. Wait a minute and I'll check the stable."

Shanna looked down at the porch steps in front of her, but the boards blended together and warned her that her depth perception was still faulty. Cautiously, she let her hand slide down the smooth pine banister as she went down the three steps.

"Holly? Jiggs?"

No answer.

Her voice rose, and she called louder than before. She could hear the faint roar of the mountain stream just over the next rise, and her heartbeat accelerated. She had told Holly to stay close to the house. Surely she wouldn't wander off as far as the creek.

"No sign of her around the stable," Marla said, hurrying back. "Maybe she decided to take a walk down the road. Or she could have gone the other direction ... toward the stream."

"That's what I'm afraid of," Shanna said anxiously.

"Then I'll start in that direction. You stay here and—"

"No, I want to come. I have sharp hearing. If she and Jiggs are playing somewhere, I'll hear them."

"Okay, give me your hand. There's an easy path running from the back of the house, down to the water's edge."

As they got closer to the creek, Shanna doubted that any child's cries could be heard above the plunging roar of the cascading water. If only she could see more than just vague impressions of trees. She knew how her daughter liked to dig in the dirt and make stick houses. She'd spent hours on the hill behind the house.

Holly might be playing anywhere nearby. *I should have watched her closer,* Shanna thought with a mother's sense of guilt.

"No sign of her," Marla said, looking up- and downstream when they reached the water's edge.

Shanna's head threatened to burst from rising terror as she shouted, "Holly...Holly!"

"She might be just around the next bend in the stream," Marla said loudly. "You stay here. Don't move. I don't want to have to fish you out of the water when I get back."

If Holly had fallen into the stream— "Hurry," she croaked. "Sit down here." The nurse eased Shanna down on a large boulder. "And wait."

With her hands pressed against the hard rock, Shanna stared at glittering waters constantly changing in her faulty vision like liquid sculptures. With a cry, she closed her eyes and buried her face in her hands. "Dear God," she prayed, "please keep Holly safe. Don't—"

The prayer was never finished. Her head jerked up when she sensed a presence behind her, but it was too late. She cried out as the back of her head exploded in pain. A thousand jagged pieces of consciousness spun away into utter darkness as she tumbled forward at the water's edge.

Chapter Thirteen

Marla found Holly downstream, skipping merrily along on the opposite bank, dangerously close to where rocks spanned the stream in a series of treacherous rapids. Ariel's protective presence had prevented the little girl from stumbling more than once on the rough ground and from pitching headfirst into the water when she had tottered on the slippery logs, following Jiggs across the stream.

"Holly! Holly!" Marla waved at the little girl. How on earth had the child gotten to the other side of the creek?

Holly didn't hear Marla hollering or see her waving. She was intent upon scrambling on all fours up a huge boulder that stuck out over the water. But Jiggs perked up his ears and ran down to the edge of the water. He barked and waved his tail furiously as he saw Marla on the other side.

Good dog, Ariel praised. *Keep it up.* She welcomed Marla's appearance. Human resources had arrived. Between the two of them they ought to be able to get Holly away from the treacherous water and back home where she belonged.

When Holly finally reached the top of the boulder wet with spray from the creek, she stood up and looked around like a princess surveying her kingdom. When she saw Marla, her face broke into a beaming smile and, tottering precariously on the uneven rock, she waved furiously.

At first the nurse just stood there looking across the plunging water, and Ariel wondered if she had even noticed the fallen logs a few yards upstream. She seemed at a loss as to how to reach the little girl and get her back on the right side of the stream.

Only one way to do it, determined Ariel. *Jiggs would have to show Marla where they'd crossed the stream.*

In the middle of an excited bark, she slipped an invisible leash around his neck. At a speed that sent his little legs flying, she urged him back to the place where the logs lay across the water. His paws hit the largest dead trunk only a few times, and a moment later he was leaping and slobbering all over Marla. As he bounded along, keeping pace with Marla on the other bank, Holly slid down from the boulder and began to retrace her steps.

When they reached the fallen log, Jiggs bounded across the gushing torrent of water once again, this time greeting Holly with enthusiastic leaps and a lapping tongue.

"Stupid dog," swore Marla. "He's going to push her in if she doesn't fall of her own accord. Jiggs, come here."

For the fourth time, the little dog bounded across the trunk bridge. With little caution and at a dangerous pace, Holly followed the dog across the log without paying any attention to her footing.

Careful, warned Ariel as Holly bounded after Jiggs. *Watch your step.* The warning went unheeded. One minute Holly was upright on a log, and the next, falling headfirst toward the water.

Even before Marla's brain could register what she was seeing, Ariel swept under Holly and set her back on the log. Her practice of pushing Jiggs off a chair and catching him before he hit the ground had paid off, after all.

"You're a naughty girl," Marla scolded after Holly had made it the rest of the way across safely and the nurse had her hands on the truant. "We've wasted half the morning looking for you. Come along. I'm going to march you right back to your mother."

Ariel left them walking back upstream. Assured of Holly's safety and propelled by an unusual awareness of earthly time passing, she spirited away to find Jay, filled with a need to connect with her human ally.

JAY HAD WAITED until the ambulance left with the McIntyre boy before he headed back to Westridge. One of the twelve-year-old's hands was badly mangled, but Jay had been able to control the bleeding, head off possible infection with an antibiotic injection, and ease the youth's pain with a sedative. He tried to reassure the frightened mother and father that their boy was going to be all right. Looking at the injury, Jay was hopeful that a surgeon would be able to reconstruct the hand with a series of operations.

Working in a nonhospital setting had been strangely exhilarating, Jay had thought as he got ready to leave. For the first time, he understood what his father meant by hands-on field medicine. No time for extensive tests. No corps of experts. Just a patient in crisis and only one physician's skill in the balance.

Heady stuff, thought Jay. And a little frightening, too. As he examined these new feelings, he was confronted with a different focus on himself and his career. Since medical school, he'd immersed himself in the frantic pace of a metropolitan hospital and big-city life. And if the truth were known, he'd never understood why a young doctor would choose any other service. But as he knelt beside the injured boy in a newly plowed field, he'd felt touched by something greater than himself. Until that moment, he'd been blind to the challenges and unaware of the drama that lay in a small town and rural practice. There had been a close involvement with the boy and his family, a contrast to an impersonal flow through a metropolitan hospital.

He frowned. Could it be that Dr. Jay Harrison was at the point of entertaining a different vision of himself, a vision that encompassed a different life-style as a doctor...and as a husband and father? As unbelievable as it was, the time he'd spent in Westridge had cleared away the debris of his compulsive, frantic existence. His frown eased into a smile and he drew in a slow, relaxing breath. "You tried to tell me, Dad. I guess I'm a slow learner about some things."

Ariel beamed at his admission. Truth and love really could work miracles, she thought with a smug smile. The handsome doctor was being honest with himself about a lot of things. Good medicine, she thought, and giggled aloud.

Jay turned and looked at the empty seat beside him. In the slanted rays of sunlight, he could almost see a beautiful blond-headed girl laughing at him. He felt her presence, her love, and as she lingered in his vision for a millisecond, he gave an embarrassed laugh at the foolish fantasy.

When Jay reached Westridge, he decided to stop at the clinic to replace the items that he'd used from his medical bag. No telling when and where he might need a full cache of drugs. Just as Jay got out of the car, he saw Skaggs come out of the café across the street and start down the sidewalk toward his office.

"Deputy!" Jay called, and hurried across the street to meet him.

Good, thought Ariel. She couldn't have arranged things better. She wanted Jay to tell him about their visit to Lew Walker's place.

Skaggs chewed on a toothpick and gave Jay only the briefest of nods. He shifted impatiently on his thick legs and cowboy boots. "What's on your mind, Doc?"

"Have you gotten back the autopsy report on Janet Rendell?"

Skaggs gave a curt nod of his head. "Yep."

"And—?"

"Well, now, I reckon that's police business." He shifted the toothpick in his pudgy mouth and leered at Jay.

"I agree, but as the physician who examined the body at the time of death, I'm sure your superiors will give me the results if you won't. Now, what did they find? Or shall I give Sheriff Dunbar a call?"

The way a ruddy flush started up Skaggs's thick neck, Jay guessed that the deputy's authority had taken a beating at the hands of his superior. Dunbar must have laid down some new rules. Skaggs's lack of competence might even cost him his job. Jay knew the man would rather sink his fist into his face than answer his questions.

Skaggs growled, "There ain't nothing in that report that you need to know. You're enough of a pain in the butt as it is. I'm telling you, Doctor, keep your nose out of my business."

"Why don't I stop in at the office and read the report myself?"

The deputy's scowl deepened like a storm about to break. "I told you, it's police business."

"I don't think Janet died from blows from a horse's hooves. I think she was dead before her mare touched her."

"You know a hell of a lot for someone who just happens to be a bystander," Skaggs flung in an accusing tone.

"So how did Janet die?"

"You tell me, big-city doctor," he said with a sneer.

"All right. She was killed by a blow to the head from something other than a horseshoe before she was thrown in the stall. Then the murderer used something hot, like a soldering gun, to torment the mare into trampling the body."

"Keep talking. You and that Ryan woman could be in this together. Wouldn't be surprised if you ended up with a noose around your own neck. We still don't know why your ladylove's album showed up at the murder scene."

"Neither do I. But I can't help but feel that the book's tied into the crime. Have you talked to Billie Jo and her boyfriend? And what does Ted have to say about his wife's autopsy?"

"I ain't saying anything more." Skaggs set his jaw.

Jay changed tactics. "I was up at Lew's place last night and saw all those junk cars. He's got just about everything a mechanic would need in that shed of his. Plenty of know-how there about repairing a car...or sabotaging one. He could have easily fixed Shanna's car so the accelerator would jam, and the guy had plenty of inflammable stuff to set her house on fire. I'm not saying he did, but you sure as hell ought to look into the possibility."

"Why in the hell would Lew or anyone else try to put the Ryan woman out of the way?"

"Probably for the same reason Janet Rendell was killed."

"I suppose you've got that figured out, too," Skaggs said sarcastically.

"Not yet," admitted Jay.

When we know why—we'll know who, Ariel added silently.

"I think you'd better stick to handing out pills, Doctor. Or maybe you're needing some shrink to take a good look at what goes on in that harebrained skull of yours." Skaggs stalked off, leaving Jay mentally making pointed comments about the deputy's own deficient brainpower.

Ariel was disappointed. Why couldn't Skaggs see what was going on right under his own nose?

Jay let himself into the clinic and knocked on Marla's apartment door. Ariel could have told him she wasn't home. Wait until he learned about Holly's escapade that morning. Marla would probably give him an earful.

Holly was going to need a firm hand, and Ariel was saddened that the communication between her and the little girl had broken down. Sadly enough, that was what happened with most children as they grew older. Holly's fantasy of a pretend playmate would fade from her mind, and Ariel knew that being her guardian angel would never be the same.

Jay spent a few minutes in the dispensary, opening cupboards and replacing the medications he'd used that morning. He closed up his bag and decided to call and tell Shanna he was on his way.

He let the phone ring a long time, but no one answered. *I wonder where they are,* he puzzled, and felt a momentary spurt of uneasiness until he reminded himself that they wouldn't hear the phone if they were outside.

He grabbed his bag and was nearly out of the office when the phone rang on the reception desk. When he answered, a pleasant, feminine voice asked to speak to Marla.

"I'm sorry, she's not here right now. May I take a message?"

"This is Dr. Stratton's office. Since Marla didn't keep her dentist appointment last Saturday, we were wondering if she'd like to reschedule?"

"I don't know. I'll have her call you." Jay hung up and scribbled a note. "Dr. Stratton's office. Call for new appointment."

He put the message on her desk and was about to turn away when the note was suddenly lifted off the desk. It sailed around his head and then fluttered down slowly to the floor, right in front of his feet.

As he picked up the note, the words he'd written leaped off the paper at him. The receptionist's voice echoed in his ears, *Since she didn't keep her dentist appointment on Saturday.*

"But she did keep it," he argued with himself, remembering that Marla had said she didn't want to wait weeks for another one. Why would she lie about a visit to the dentist? Maybe she didn't want to admit she was chicken about having someone work on her teeth, he reasoned, but nothing about Marla suggested that she had an ounce of cowardice in her body. There was probably a simple explanation, but, puzzled by an insistence that defied comprehension, he dialed his father's number.

"Hi, Dad, it's me. Just got back from a call and—"

His father wanted to know who and what. Jay explained as quickly as he could about the McIntyre boy. Any other time he would have shared with his father the satisfaction he'd experienced that morning, but at the moment his thoughts were centered on something else.

"Did Marla stop by and see you when she was in Denver night before last? Saturday night?"

His father chuckled. "What are you doing, checking up on the old man's love life?"

"Not a bit. Believe me, the question has nothing to do with your romantic assignations, Dad. I'm just interested in checking out something."

"I don't understand. What's so important about whether Marla and I got together last weekend."

"Marla said she stayed overnight in Denver after her dentist appointment on Saturday. I just want to know if she was with you."

"I haven't the foggiest idea what you're after, but no, I haven't seen Marla for a week or two. I've talked to her on the phone. In fact, she called me last night, and we talked for a long time about you and Shanna

Ryan. Doesn't take a brain surgeon to know what's going on in that direction. I hope that—"

"We'll talk about that later," Jay said shortly.

"No, I want to know what this call is all about. What's got you in a knot about Marla?"

"I don't really know. It's just that Marla must have lied to me about the dentist and I don't understand why."

"It's really none of your business whether she came to Denver or not. I mean, what difference does it make?"

"Probably none at all."

While Jay was talking to his father, Ariel invaded Marla's apartment with a speed of a lightning flash. As she sped through the rooms, she viewed drawers and closets without finding anything but the most pragmatic of belongings. Everything in the nurse's small living quarters matched her no-nonsense personality.

The only thing that seemed aesthetic at all was a small curio cabinet set in the corner of her bedroom. Small Chinese figurines sat on glass shelf, and a lovely lacquered box placed on the bottom grabbed Ariel's attention. She could tell that it had been moved recently because of the faint dust marks.

Quickly Ariel eased the box out of the cabinet and set it on the floor. Was it Marla's "hidey box," as Holly called the cigar box where she carefully kept secret possessions? Even the most practical people often gave into the urge to secrete away private belongings.

The small lock was no challenge, and in an instant Ariel had the lid up and the contents spread out on the floor. The missing photos from Shanna's album were on top. Three of them. In each one a smiling blond nurse in a hospital nursery held up an infant for the camera. Written on the back were the words, "Nurse Edith Evans and Holly Ryan, one day old."

Nurse Edith Evans's plump figure and round face hadn't changed much in five years, and the woman in the photos was easily recognizable as Marla Dillard.

A yellowed newspaper article lay at the bottom of the box. The headline read, Army Nurse Charged With Manslaughter Disappears. The account stated that two women patients at the Fort Benning medical facility had died as the result of a registered nurse, Edith Evans, administering the wrong medication while under the influence of an illegal drug. The accused was ordered to stand trial, but before she could be brought to court, Edith Evans broke her bond and disappeared.

In the other room, Jay was trying to get off the phone. "I don't have time to explain, Dad. I have to look into something."

"Wait a minute. Tell me what in the hell is going on?"

"Dad, I—"

At that moment, Ariel sent the wooden box sailing into the cabinet. The glass door shattered into a thousand jagged pieces.

"What the—?" Jay hung up the phone and ran into Marla's apartment. He stopped in the doorway of her living room, stunned by glass lying everywhere and the curio door hanging half off. Then his eyes fell on the three photos and newspaper clipping scattered on the floor in front of him.

The light in the room shifted.

A roar of wings sounded in his ears.

Shaken by sensations he didn't understand, he bent over and picked up the scattered photos and clipping. As he held them in his hand, all the pieces of the puzzle came crashing together.

With terrifying certainty, he knew where the danger to Shanna lay.

Chapter Fourteen

Shanna's cheek scraped against the harshness of splintered wood as she floated back to consciousness. As murky darkness swirled around her, she was caught in a weird sensation of being underwater. She could hear the lapping and sucking of water, and she shivered from a cold mist that laid a chill upon her. She felt the weight of humid black air like a damp shroud covering her.

Groans sounded distant in her own ears, even though she knew they were coming from her parched mouth. As strength flowed back into her trembling body, she tried to get up. As she pressed against rough wood and raised herself into a sitting position, sharp tiny splinters bit into her hands, tendrils of hair fell over her face, and the damp, dusty smell of mildew assaulted her nostrils. Sitting hunched over, dizzy and disoriented, she gingerly touched a warm, moist spot on the back of her head.

Blood.

She put her hands up to her temples and struggled to pull jagged pieces of memory from the swirling cauldron of her brain. She'd been by the creek. She searched her hazy memory. Had she fallen? Hit her head? Wandered in a daze into this place looking for Holly?

Holly!

A stab of panic blotted out all other thoughts and sent adrenaline surging through her.

I have to find Holly.

She wavered to her feet and then froze. A possessive darkness flowed around her, and she was unable to take a step forward. Her heart raced wildly as she gingerly turned her head in every direction. She couldn't see anything. Where was she? The boards under her feet sagged with her weight, and even though she couldn't see the water, she knew it was there.

She went back down to her knees. A fusty smell of dank wood and rotting vegetation filled her nostrils. Leaning forward on her knees, she blindly let her hand slide across the splintery boards in front of her before she cautiously moved forward, inches at a time.

Like a trapped animal in a maze, she had barely moved a few feet when her way was blocked. She couldn't tell if she'd reached a wall or wooden door. Turning in another direction, she continued to feel her way and crawl forward. Suddenly she jerked back. At first, she didn't believe it. Her exploring had felt nothing but open air.

The dank, rotting floorboards had disappeared.

For a long moment, she couldn't move. She froze on her knees. If she hadn't been feeling her way along, she would have crawled off into the empty space and down into the sucking water below. Thank God the caution she'd learned from her limited vision had saved her. And she was becoming oriented in the cavelike surroundings. She had made a mental note of where the wall had stopped her and where the open space in the floor lay.

Turning slowly on her knees in another direction, she crawled slowly forward again. This time there was no impediment to her movement and she must have crawled at least ten feet, she determined, when the thick blackness surrounding her was suddenly broken by shafts of splintered light.

She blinked as her pupils adjusted to the change. She realized that she must have crawled out of a confined space. Her vision wasn't sharp enough to distinguish the height and breadth of the bigger area. She let her eyes follow a pattern of light and dark until her gaze settled on an opening that was almost recognizable as a doorway.

As she stared at it, she realized with a bound of joy that the silhouette of a person was clearly framed in the opening.

MARLA'S JEEP WAS STILL parked in front of the cabin when Ariel swept through the door, fanning the air with a swish of invisible wings. How long ago had she left Holly in Marla's hands? As always, time was a trial to the little angel. She just couldn't fathom minutes and hours. And yet, she knew that such mortal measurements could mean the difference between pain and happiness, success and failure.

What had the nurse done with the child?

Ariel feared that Marla Dillard, aka Edith Evans, was a woman desperate enough to sacrifice another human life to keep her identity a secret. Janet Rendell must have seen the photos in the album, and Marla had arranged the woman's death to silence her. One thing was certain. The frightened nurse had nothing to lose by adding more victims to her treachery.

Ariel went through the small house in a flash. A building apprehension dissolved in a flash of joy when she found Holly was curled up asleep with Jiggs at her feet. Ariel was so relieved that she brushed a whispered angel kiss on the little girl's cheek.

Holly stirred and then smiled in her sleep. The child's breathing was easy and natural. Not drugged, thank heavens. Just worn-out from her morning escapade. Holly was okay.

But what about Shanna?

The figure in the doorway came closer. "Help," Shanna croaked. "Help."

"Well, look at you," Marla answered in her usual brisk tone.

"Oh, Marla, thank God." Hysterical relief sluiced through Shanna as she let herself go limp. She remained sitting on the floor, because her legs felt too weak to hold. She wanted to cry, and laugh at the same time. Then her thoughts swirled away from her own safety. She gasped, "Holly? Did you find Holly."

"She was playing downstream. I took her back to the house and put her down for a nap."

"Thank God," breathed Shanna. She touched her hand to the wound on the back of her head. "I don't know if I fell or something hit me and knocked me out. Where am I?"

"The old mill. I'm surprised Jay didn't take you for a scenic walk along the creek and tell you about it. It's not far from the house. Lots of people take pictures of the picturesque waterwheel and its hanging buckets." Marla explained as if she had nothing more important to do at the moment than be a tourist guide.

Shanna remembered Jay describing some of the leftover relics of Westridge's past, which included an old mill, but she hadn't paid any attention to where it was located. "How'd I get here?"

Marla stood over her. "I brought you."

"You brought me," Shanna echoed as her logical mind searched for a plausible reason.

"You were out like a light when I left you here...and I thought you'd stay that way until I got back. You really are tougher all around than I had expected."

Shanna couldn't make any sense out of what Marla was saying. "You brought me here?"

"You're going to have another accident, Shanna. And this one is going to be your last."

As Shanna looked up at the shadowy figure, she rejected what her mind was telling her. It couldn't be. The nurse was a friend. Someone who had helped her to cope. *Your next accident will kill you.* "Not you, Marla."

"I warned you to leave Westridge," she answered in her brisk manner. "And I can't risk any more time. Not with your sight improving every day. There's too much at stake. Once you get a clear look at me, you'll remember."

"Remember?"

"You do remember Edith Evans, don't you?"

Shanna's forehead furrowed as the name flickered in the recesses of her memory. "Edith Evans? Edith Evans? Oh, now I remember. The army nurse that killed those people? And then disappeared before they brought her to trial—" Shanna broke off.

"That's the one," Marla said flatly. "You do remember what Edith looked like, don't you? In fact, you had some photos of her holding your new baby. Your husband took them, remember. Nice clear snapshots. No problem recognizing the nurse. None at all. Just ask Janet. She was snooping around my place, found the album that I'd taken from your house, and she carried it off. I had to kill her after she told me she'd hidden it in the barn."

Shanna was too stunned to answer. Like dry leaves whipped by a devil's wind, the unbelievable truth fell into place. Marla Dillard was Edith Evans. She remembered the woman clearly now. The newspapers had been filled with the ugly story of the manslaughter charges brought against the nurse and her disappearance five years ago.

"I can't believe it," Shanna said more to herself than the woman standing over her.

"Too bad, you turned up in my corner of the world. I have a good thing going here. Nobody questions my new name and false credentials. I have a good life here, and it's going to get even better. You see, I plan on marrying Dr. Bradley Harrison."

Shanna swallowed hard. "Someone will find out about you. You can't hide forever."

Marla gave a short laugh. "Maybe not, but I'm not concerned about forever. I'll take things as they come. Right now, you're the one threatening my future."

"You'll never get away with another accident," Shanna said bravely.

"That's where you're wrong. Your blindness has played right into my hands. Lucky for you or I would have had to move much faster. No one is going to believe that you didn't wander into here by yourself. And not being able to see clearly—" She shrugged.

"Jay will know better."

"But he isn't here, is he." She reached down and grabbed Shanna's arm. "That's enough talk. The water runs deep under this old building. Falling through the floor while hunting for your little girl could keep your body from surfacing for a long time."

Shanna broke Marla's grip. Crawling backward, she retreated in the only direction open to her—the dark recess where she had been before. Once more she was enveloped in a murky darkness with open floorboards on both sides of her.

"Good, Shanna," Marla encouraged as she followed her. "Keep moving. Save me the trouble of having to push you off into the water."

Shanna tried to remember how far she had crawled earlier before she reached the end of the sagging boards. At the time, she'd made a mental picture of the floor—only a couple of more feet before the boards ran out.

"That's it. Keep going," urged Marla, prodding her with the tip of her shoe. She dogged Shanna's every crawling inch backward. "Just a little farther."

Shanna knew that if she tried to stand up, her unsteady balance would make it easy for Marla to give her a deadly shove. But if she stayed on her hands and knees until the floorboards ran out, Marla could still shove her into the watery abyss.

Shanna stopped moving and raised her head to the shadowy figure poised over her. "Marla, please . . ." she begged.

Grab her around the knees!

A sudden blanket of warmth came with the order, as if some unseen presence was there with her. The voice was so clear that Shanna didn't hesitate. She lifted her arms and flung them around Marla's legs.

Her hold was at the right height to lock her arms behind Marla's knees.

Pull!

Shanna jerked her locked arms, and Marla's legs buckled as her knees bent. As she struggled to right herself, she fell backward on the sagging floorboards. A loud splintering and crackling filled the air. Decaying boards gave way under the top half of her and then threatened to slide the rest of her body down into swirling black water.

"Pull me up! Pull me up," Marla cried as her arms flayed out in every direction.

Shanna couldn't keep hold of Marla's bent knees, so she let loose and grabbed her ankles and tried to keep the nurse from sliding forward on the slanted boards.

Hold on.

Shanna obeyed the inner voice, even though the nurse's weight was pulling her inch by threatening inch toward the jagged hole and the black waters swirling beneath.

JAY HAD BROKEN EVERY speed limit getting back to Deerview, and now he screeched to a stop in front of the house. Marla's Jeep was still parked there, and he raced inside, ready to confront her.

Jiggs came bounding out of the bedroom, waving his tail in friendly welcome.

Holly was asleep in her bed. There was no sign of Shanna and Marla.

Jay grabbed the phone.

"Deputy's office," Skaggs answered in his slow drawl.

Jay hurriedly identified himself and then said, "Get a search party and get over to my place—now! Marla Dillard is our murderer and she must have Shanna." He slammed down the receiver before Skaggs could say anything and raced out the door.

He sprinted toward the creek with intuitive compulsion. The roar of plunging waters matched the hammering of his heartbeat. Marla had tried at least twice to kill Shanna and had failed. A drowning accident could be easily arranged.

"Shanna! Shanna!" Her name was like a war cry as he raced along the banks, and he was downstream a few yards from the deserted mill when the old waterwheel that had been silent for decades began to turn.

He froze as his brain registered the impossible. The old building was in shambles. There was no way the broken wheel could be turning.

I must be hallucinating.

He stared at the unbelievable sight of filling and emptying buckets. The walls and roof of the mill were scarcely more than a pile of weathered timbers hanging over the water. The old wheel sagged with broken spokes. It couldn't be turning—but it was!

He broke into a run and bounded into the dark recesses of the old mill. His eyes strained to focus in the darkened gloom as he pushed his way into a cavelike enclosure of fallen timbers without any thought of his own safety.

"Shanna!"

He heard a muffled cry, but he couldn't see her as he made his way through a maze of listing timbers. The sound of flowing water came clearly through jagged holes in the sagging floor. "Where are you?"

His heart lurched to a stop when he heard Marla's shrill cry. "Help... help."

Marla! Such rage rose in his chest that he knew he was capable of savage revenge if she'd already harmed Shanna.

Following Marla's shrieks, he made his way across the sagging floorboards into a cavern made by fallen timbers. In the murky darkness he could barely make out two figures on the floor in front of him.

"Shanna?"

"I can't... hold her... much longer."

He fell down at her side. "What the—?" He saw then that Shanna was clutching Marla's ankles to keep the rest of her from sliding into the watery hole.

Marla cried out as he took a firm hold of her feet. The rugged edge of the boards scraped her hips and back as he pulled her off the slanting boards only inches from the water below. Marla sat up just as the weakened floorboards creaked a warning.

"Let's get out of here! The whole thing is going to give way." Jay pulled Shanna up, put his arm around her waist and guided her back through fallen timbers and listing walls. He didn't wait to see if Marla was following.

Ariel returned the old waterwheel to its dilapidated state. The old mill had served its purpose. The sight of filling and emptying buckets had brought Jay running to the mill. He had recognized the signal of danger.

A glare of sunshine greeted Jay and Shanna as they emerged from the dark interior of the mill. He pulled Shanna into his arms, his eyes moist with thankfulness as he searched her precious face. "Are you all right?"

Before she could answer, Marla said briskly, "Of course, Shanna's all right. What a dumb thing she did wandering into that old building looking for Holly. I nearly lost my life trying to save her."

Both Shanna and Jay looked at the woman as if they'd never known or seen her before. This was not the administering nurse they had taken for a friend.

They didn't know her. They had never known her.

"It's over," Jay said finally. "It's all over, Edith."

Chapter Fifteen

When Ariel flashed into the outer office of the Denver Branch of Avenging Angels on Logan Street, the white-clad receptionist, Grace, looked up and smiled. "Well, hello there, Ariel. We've been hearing good things about you." The gray-haired angel beamed. "You handled your first Avenging Angel mission very well. Are you back for your next assignment?"

"No. I don't want one."

Grace's clear blue eyes widened. She looked almost shocked at Ariel's blunt answer. "You don't want one?"

"No."

"Of course you do. That's the way of things." Her voice took on a lecturing tone. "Angels are meant to serve God and humans as best they can. When one mission is successfully concluded, another assignment is made. The state of mankind is a constant challenge to all of us." Then her tone softened. "Are you worried that you won't be the little girl's Guardian Angel any more? That's not for you to decide, you know. You've done very well, but it may be time for you to move on to another family."

"I don't want another family."

Grace sighed. A little bit of success had certainly created a boldness in Ariel that was extremely displeasing. Humility and meekness were Grace's favorite angelic traits, and she feared this child angel had lost a good measure of them. Well, Angelo would have to handle the matter. She was grateful that there was a heavenly hierarchy to handle every situation. Her sense of rightness restored, Grace said pleasantly, "I'm sure Angelo will be delighted to see you."

Ariel wasn't so sure. His booming greeting when she appeared in front of the magnificent Italian angel was less than reassuring. "I've been expecting you."

"You have?"

"Certainly." His craggy face softened. "You handled all three of your angel assignments very well."

"Three?"

"Guarding, Avenging, and you threw in Cupid for good measure." His luminous smile filled the room. "Not only did you keep your little girl and her mother from harm, but you successfully guided your human sleuthing partner in finding the empirical evidence needed for bringing the killer to justice. And in addition, you gave unconditional love to this family, and in so doing opened up new avenues for them."

"That's what I want to talk to you about," Ariel said bravely.

"I know," Angelo said as he laced his strong fingers together on the desk. "And I've been thinking a lot about what you're going to ask. God made man a little lower than the angels. Lower, Ariel. Do you understand what that means?"

"I think so. Angels don't have to go through all the stuff that humans do."

"Stuff?"

"You know—pain, hurting and dying." Then her little pugnacious chin came out. "But they can laugh and sing and hold each other. They can feel love. A baby can be kissed and cuddled and—"

"Is that what this is about, Ariel?"

She nodded. "Holly has a daddy now... and she wants a baby sister. They all want this love child that will bring joy to their lives. And... and I want to be a part of their happiness."

"You want to change your spiritual status so that you can be that little sister?"

"Yes... yes. That would be wonderful."

"I don't think you understand, Ariel, that most angels consider returning to earthly bonds as a kind of punishment. Not a reward for services rendered."

She returned his steady gaze. Her clear blue eyes twinkled at him. "I guess not even angels are all alike."

A faint smile crossed his lips. "Perhaps not." He shrugged his massive shoulders. "Request granted."

SHANNA SAW JAY'S HOPEFUL expression as they followed the lady real-estate agent up the steps of a Swiss chalet overlooking picturesque Cedarville. She knew what he was thinking: *Maybe this is the one.* As she looked into Jay's loving face, she knew that she had been blessed beyond belief and the miracle of sight was something she would never take for granted again.

The week after they were married, Jay had given his notice at Manhattan General and had begun the process of setting up his general practice in Cedarville. Jay's decision to stay in Colorado had helped his dad weather the truth about Marla.

"I just can't believe it." His father had been shaken to the core. "Her credentials looked authentic. I know you can buy things like that, but I never had any reason to question hers. She was a competent nurse. I never saw any signs of substance abuse."

"She probably went clean after what happened. If she had stayed and faced the manslaughter charges instead of fleeing, she might have been able to put her life back together. Now she's facing first-degree murder charges."

"I can't help but feel sorry for her," Bradley Harrison said. "Such a waste. I . . . I really was fond of her."

"And maybe that's one of the main reasons she did what she did. She couldn't bear to give up the chance she had for a new beginning with you. When she saw Shanna and realized that she would recognize her if they ever came face-to-face, she panicked. She learned a lot about vehicles while in the army and fixed the accelerator on Shanna's car. Only the arranged accident wasn't fatal—but the injury to Shanna's eyes gave her more time to arrange something else."

"The fire," Bradley Harrison said sadly.

"And when that didn't work, she knew time was running out. I'm just thankful that she didn't have the heart to hurt Holly. It was only Shanna who was the danger, no one else—until Janet Rendell was snooping around Marla's and found the photo album that Marla had seen when she was helping move Shanna's things downstairs. I walked her to the door that night, so she didn't have a chance to take it then, but she swiped one of the spare keys hanging in the kitchen and came back after the album in the middle of the night."

"But why did the Rendell woman hide it in the barn?"

"Jan probably thought that was as good a hiding place as any, but Marla must have threatened her enough that she showed her where it was. And that was Janet's mistake. Marla knew that Janet wouldn't rest until she knew why Marla's picture was in it. So she had to kill her.

"They found horseshoe clippers that had been washed and put back on Ted's workbench. Marla must have struck Janet in the head, put her in the stall with her horse and then jabbed Lady with a hot soldering iron to make her rear and stomp."

"I wonder why she left the photo album there?"

"To incriminate Janet, no doubt. Marla took the pages that had the photographs of her holding Holly and left the rest. Why Marla kept them, I don't know. Maybe a part of her wanted someone to understand why she'd been forced to do what she did." Jay felt sorry for his father and was glad that Shanna and Holly had become good medicine for him.

After Dr. Harrison, senior, got acquainted with Shanna, he told his son that it was about time he got some sense about what life was all about.

Jay had agreed.

The sale of Shanna's property to Ted Rendell had gone smoothly. He had decided to carry out Jan's wishes and build a lodge where the old house had stood. In the hope that Billie Jo might take hold and find some purpose in her life, he'd given her some say-so in the new venture.

Shanna had realized enough of a down payment from the sale to invest in a B and B in Cedarville. Every day she and Jay looked at property that might fulfill Shanna's determination to succeed as a businesswoman. Both of them loved the picturesque mountain town, and since it was located near one of Colorado's most popular resorts, a prosperous business year-round was almost a certainty.

As they walked through the eight-bedroom chalet, an old-world charm greeted them. Polished open beams, intricately carved staircases, copper fixtures gleaming with a burnished glow, and hand-loomed rugs and hangings; all created a sense of quiet leisure.

And when they walked out on a balcony and looked below at Holly and Jiggs playing on a small terrace, a thrill traveled up Shanna's spine.

"What do you think?" Jay asked.

"It's . . . it's too perfect."

Whenever her face lit up like that, he wanted to take her in his arms and kiss her senseless. "I take it you like it."

"I like it."

"Good. So do I. Come on, let's take another look around."

They went through the chalet once more, this time with the perspective of new owners, and when they showed Holly the room she was going to have, she was excited about having a big, grown-up bed for the first time.

"What about the baby?" Holly asked as she bounced down on the full-sized bed.

Shanna and Jay exchanged puzzled glances. Shanna was only a few weeks' pregnant, and they hadn't talked to Holly about the coming addition to their family. They had decided to wait until they were settled.

"She'll need a bed. Where's my baby sister going to sleep?"

"Probably in the small room next to yours," Shanna answered as evenly as she could. This was a conversation she had never expected. Her little daughter constantly threw her off-balance. "We'll have to buy some new furniture for a nursery."

"Pink and white. That's what girls like. Blue for boys. Pink for girls."

"How do know the baby's going to be a girl?"

Holly's little mouth curved in a wise smile. "I just know." Then she giggled. "I even know what her name is going to be."

And in that moment of wondrous heavenly insight, Jay and Shanna also knew her name.

Weddings by DeWilde

Since the turn of the century the elegant and fashionable DeWilde stores have helped brides around the world turn the fantasy of their "Special Day" into reality. But now the store and three generations of family are torn apart by the divorce of Grace and Jeffrey DeWilde. As family members face new challenges and loves—and a long-secret mystery—the lives of Grace and Jeffrey intermingle with store employees, friends and relatives in this fast-paced, glamorous, internationally set series. For weddings and romance, glamour and fun-filled entertainment, enter the world of DeWilde . . .

Twelve remarkable books, coming to you once a month, beginning in April 1996

Weddings by DeWilde begins with
Shattered Vows
by Jasmine Cresswell

Here's a preview!

"SPEND THE NIGHT with me, Lianne."

No softening lies, no beguiling promises, just the curt offer of a night of sex. She closed her eyes, shutting out temptation. She had never expected to feel this sort of relentless drive for sexual fulfillment, so she had no mechanisms in place for coping with it. "No." The one-word denial was all she could manage to articulate.

His grip on her arms tightened as if he might refuse to accept her answer. Shockingly, she wished for a split second that he would ignore her rejection and simply bundle her into the car and drive her straight to his flat, refusing to take no for an answer. All the pleasures of mindless sex, with none of the responsibility. For a couple of seconds he neither moved nor spoke. Then he released her, turning abruptly to open the door on the passenger side of his Jaguar. "I'll drive you home," he said, his voice hard and flat. "Get in."

The traffic was heavy, and the rain started again as an annoying drizzle that distorted depth perception made driving difficult, but Lianne didn't fool herself that the silence inside the car was caused by the driving conditions. The air around them crackled and sparked with their thwarted desire. Her body was still on fire. Why didn't Gabe say something? she thought, feeling aggrieved.

Perhaps because he was finding it as difficult as she was to think of something appropriate to say. He was thirty years old, long past the stage of needing to bed a woman just so he could record another sexual conquest in his little black book. He'd spent five months dating Julia, which suggested he was a man who valued friendship as an element in his relationships with women. Since he didn't seem to like her very much, he was probably as embarrassed as she was by the stupid, inexplicable intensity of their physical response to each other.

"Maybe we should just set aside a weekend to have wild, uninterrupted sex," she said, thinking aloud. "Maybe that way we'd get whatever it is we feel for each other out of our systems and be able to move on with the rest of our lives."

His mouth quirked into a rueful smile. "Isn't that supposed to be my line?"

"Why? Because you're the man? Are you sexist enough to believe that women don't have sexual urges? I'm just as aware of what's going on between us as you are, Gabe. Am I supposed to pretend I haven't noticed that we practically ignite whenever we touch? And that we have nothing much in common except mutual lust—and a good friend we betrayed?"

HARLEQUIN®

Don't miss these Harlequin favorites by some of our most distinguished authors!
And now, you can receive a discount by ordering two or more titles!

HT #25645	THREE GROOMS AND A WIFE by JoAnn Ross	$3.25 U.S./$3.75 CAN.	☐
HT #25648	JESSIE'S LAWMAN by Kristine Rolofson	$3.25 U.S./$3.75 CAN.	☐
HP #11725	THE WRONG KIND OF WIFE by Roberta Leigh	$3.25 U.S./$3.75 CAN.	☐
HP #11755	TIGER EYES by Robyn Donald	$3.25 U.S./$3.75 CAN.	☐
HR #03362	THE BABY BUSINESS by Rebecca Winters	$2.99 U.S./$3.50 CAN.	☐
HR #03375	THE BABY CAPER by Emma Goldrick	$2.99 U.S./$3.50 CAN.	☐
HS #70638	THE SECRET YEARS by Margot Dalton	$3.75 U.S./$4.25 CAN.	☐
HS #70655	PEACEKEEPER by Marisa Carroll	$3.75 U.S./$4.25 CAN.	☐
HI #22280	MIDNIGHT RIDER by Laura Pender	$2.99 U.S./$3.50 CAN.	☐
HI #22235	BEAUTY VS THE BEAST by M.J. Rogers	$3.50 U.S./$3.99 CAN.	☐
HAR #16531	TEDDY BEAR HEIR by Elda Minger	$3.50 U.S./$3.99 CAN.	☐
HAR #16596	COUNTERFEIT HUSBAND by Linda Randall Wisdom	$3.50 U.S./$3.99 CAN.	☐
HH #28795	PIECES OF SKY by Marianne Willman	$3.99 U.S./$4.50 CAN.	☐
HH #28855	SWEET SURRENDER by Julie Tetel	$4.50 U.S./$4.99 CAN.	☐

(limited quantities available on certain titles)

	AMOUNT	$
DEDUCT:	**10% DISCOUNT FOR 2+ BOOKS**	$
ADD:	**POSTAGE & HANDLING**	$
	($1.00 for one book, 50¢ for each additional)	
	APPLICABLE TAXES**	$_____
	TOTAL PAYABLE	$_____
	(check or money order—please do not send cash)	

To order, complete this form and send it, along with a check or money order for the total above, payable to Harlequin Books, to: **In the U.S.:** 3010 Walden Avenue, P.O. Box 9047, Buffalo, NY 14269-9047; **In Canada:** P.O. Box 613, Fort Erie, Ontario, L2A 5X3.

Name: _____

Address: _____ City: _____

State/Prov.: _____ Zip/Postal Code: _____

**New York residents remit applicable sales taxes.
Canadian residents remit applicable GST and provincial taxes.

HBACK-AJ3

MILLION DOLLAR SWEEPSTAKES
AND
EXTRA BONUS PRIZE DRAWING

No purchase necessary. To enter the sweepstakes, follow the directions published and complete and mail your Official Entry Form. If your Official Entry Form is missing, or you wish to obtain an additional one (limit: one Official Entry Form per request, one request per outer mailing envelope) send a separate, stamped, self-addressed #10 envelope (4 1/8" X 9 1/2") via first-class mail to: Million Dollar Sweepstakes and Extra Bonus Prize Drawing Entry Form, P.O. Box 1867, Buffalo, NY 14269-1867. Request must be received no later than January 15, 1998. For eligibility into the sweepstakes, entries must be received no later than March 31,1998. No liability is assumed for printing errors, lost, late, non-delivered or misdirected entries. Odds of winning are determined by the number of eligible entries distributed and received.

Sweepstakes open to residents of the U.S. (except Puerto Rico), Canada and Europe who are 18 years of age or older. All applicable laws and regulations apply. Sweepstakes offer void wherever prohibited by law. Values of all prizes are in U.S. currency. This sweepstakes is presented by Torstar Corp., its subsidiaries and affiliates, in conjunction with book, merchandise and/or product offerings. For a copy of the Official Rules governing this sweepstakes, send a self-addressed, stamped envelope (WA residents need not affix return postage) to: MILLION DOLLAR SWEEP-STAKES AND EXTRA BONUS PRIZE DRAWING Rules, P.O. Box 4470, Blair, NE 68009-4470, USA.

FAST CASH 4033 DRAW RULES
NO PURCHASE OR OBLIGATION NECESSARY

Fifty prizes of $50 each will be awarded in random drawings to be conducted no later than 6/28/96 from amongst all eligible responses to this prize offer received as of 5/14/96. To enter, follow directions, affix 1st-class postage and mail OR write Fast Cash 4033 on a 3" x 5" card along with your name and address and mail that card to: Harlequin's Fast Cash 4033 Draw, P.O. Box 1395, Buffalo, NY 14240-1395 OR P.O. Box 618, Fort Erie, Ontario L2A 5X3. (Limit: one entry per outer envelope; all entries must be sent via 1st-class mail.) Limit: one prize per household. Odds of winning are determined by the number of eligible responses received. Offer is open only to residents of the U.S. (except Puerto Rico) and Canada and is void wherever prohibited by law. All applicable laws and regulations apply. Any litigation within the province of Quebec respecting the conduct and awarding of a prize in this sweepstakes may be submitted to the Régie des alcools, des courses et des jeux. In order for a Canadian resident to win a prize, that person will be required to correctly answer a time-limited arithmetical skill-testing question to be administered by mail. Names of winners available after 7/30/96 by sending a self-addressed, stamped envelope to: Fast Cash 4033 Draw Winners, P.O. Box 4200, Blair, NE 68009-4200.

SWP-H3ZD

Weddings by DeWilde

Since the turn of the century, the elegant and fashionable DeWilde stores have helped brides around the world turn the fantasy of their "Special Day" into reality. But now the store and three generations of family are torn apart by the separation of Grace and Jeffrey DeWilde. Family members face new challenges and loves in this fast-paced, glamorous, internationally set series. For weddings and romance, glamour and fun-filled entertainment, enter the world of DeWilde...

Watch for The RELUCTANT BRIDE by Janis Flores Coming to you in May

Rita Shannon has just been hired as Grace DeWilde's executive assistant. Helping to create the new San Francisco store was a dream come true...until Rita was forced to rely on deal-maker Erik Mulholland, a man whose past betrayal still wounded her to the depths of her soul.

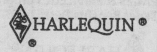

You're About to Become a
Privileged Woman

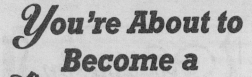

**Reap the rewards of fabulous free gifts and
benefits with proofs-of-purchase from
Harlequin and Silhouette books**

Pages & Privileges™

**It's our way of thanking you for
buying our books at your
favorite retail stores.**

PROOF OF
PURCHASE
Offer expires October 31, 1996

HI-PP128

**Harlequin and Silhouette—
the most privileged readers in the world!**

**For more information about Harlequin and
Silhouette's PAGES & PRIVILEGES program call the
Pages & Privileges Benefits Desk: 1-503-794-2499**

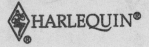

HARLEQUIN®

H1-PP128